DEATH FLEX

DEATH FLEX

Crabtree
Daker
Glover
Jackson
Johnson
Palacio
Renninger
Rhoads

Nantes   2023

This is a Bent Missile Book,
Published by Pilum Press.

Cover design and typesetting by Luisa Editorial. Copyediting and proofing by Chicago Superior. Angle d'aguisement and incidence by Infantry, the Old Guard Sleepatorium, and Rufus, superhorse.

REMEMBER: PILUM PRESS USES *ALL* THE LETTERS OF THE ALPHABET!

ISBN: 978-1-956453-09-6

Published July 2023

"At times like this I remembered a story Maman used to tell me about my father. I never knew him. Maybe the only thing I did know about the man was the story Maman would tell me back then: he'd gone to watch a murderer be executed. Just the thought of going had made him sick to his stomach. But he went anyway, and when he came back he spent half the morning throwing up. I remember feeling a little disgusted by him at the time. But now I understood, it was perfectly normal. How had I not seen that there was nothing more import-ant than an execution, and that when you come right down to it, it was the only thing a man could truly be interested in? If I ever got out of this prison I would go and watch every execution there was."

—Albert Camus, The Stranger

CONTENTS

VIEW FROM THE GALLERY

An introduction

"The thing that hath been, it is that which shall be; and that which is done is that which shall be done: and there is no new thing under the sun."

This, according to the King James version (KJV) of Ecclesiastes 1:9. This idea, even down to its approximate phrasing, was not new when the King James Bible was published in 1611, since the KJV was based on already extant English-version translations (which were a translation of a Hebrew text written sometime between 450 BCE and 180 BCE). But there's something distinct about this version: we see the (unknown) author (one of the forty-seven scholars that developed the KJV) trying to figure out both how to be true to the original concept and also shaping the verse's vocabulary, syntax, rhyme, and rhythm to make it something that, even if it has been said before, still feels distinct, still feels slightly unique. Everything has already been said before... and yet, if one is attentive to the gestures of language, to both their surface and subterranean motions, things can be said again in a way that gives them a distinct personality, in a way that makes us glad to have read them (again).

Accepting that everything has already been and already been done can be, for the right sort of writer, a source of a relief. Rather than trying to find the next new thing, rather than pursuing the endless search for novelty, you begin to understand that what makes writing good is not the uniqueness of its idea but the texture of the writing itself, the eccentricity and musicality with which the writing is rendered.

By now, you may be asking yourself, "What exactly does this have to do with *Death Flex*?"

I'm glad you asked.

The stories in *Death Flex* are responses to and/or reworkings of Franz Schmidt's *A Hangman's Diary*. They are attempts to deliberately take up the words and ideas of another writer and to see what can be made of them. Rather than running toward novelty, they run obdurately toward the idea that there is nothing new under the sun. And yet they insist that despite this constraint the nothing new can still be grounds for intriguing writing.

As a choice for something to respond to Schmidt's diary is a curious and interesting one. Franz Schmidt was the public executioner of Nuremberg from 1573 to 1617. *A Hangman's Diary* is his work journal; it consists largely of a year by year, person by person, account of those he punished or killed over the course of four decades. Often staccato, these entries sometimes offer only a little. For instance, "June 5th. Leonhardt Russ, of Ceyern, a thief, hanged at Statt Steinach. Was my first execution," reads the first entry. Other entries are even more telegraphic: four entries in 1574, 1575 and 1576 read simply "A thief hanged." without bothering to name the thief. Indeed, thirty-six of the several hundred entries in the diary say simply "A thief hanged." And no more. As a reader it's hard sometimes not to be lulled into the false sense of security that accountancy provides by this—which can make the more specific entries shocking. Kloss Renckhart of Feylsdorf, for instance, not only gets a full name and a place associated with him, we're also given the specifics of his murders. These include the fact that after he shot a miller he "did violence to the miller's wife and the maid, obliged them to fry some eggs in fat and laid these on the dead miller's body, then forced the miller's wife to join in eating them." It's wonderfully, horribly specific, and very hard to forget. Or there's the fact that Schmidt records of someone that "During the first night a pair of red knitted stockings was put on him as he hung on the gallows." Or consider the very odd and specific threat that Cuntz Rhünagel made, that first he would burn someone's house down and then "he would afterwards cut off their hands and hide them in his breast." There's a whole story hiding in that description... There's a lot, too, in the brief moments when Schmidt describes a convict as being "beheaded as a favor." Some favor...

The writers in *Death Flex* who take up the challenge of reworking Schmidt are reading him meticulously and with an open mind, looking for openings that will either spark their own imaginations or allow them to nudge Schmidt in their own direction. Brian Renninger's "Thirty-One Blows" fleshes out a few days in Schmidt's life and takes on the moment in 1585 when he was made to break his brother-in-law on the wheel. It fills in all the details the historical record leaves out, ranging from Schmidt's family life to what it's like for him to skate up the iced-over river. Lester Glover's "Maledicta" tells the story of Pony, a gambler, and his faithful but hapless companion Kuntz. The first story fills in gaps that we know exist, while the second offsets Schmidt's own account by narrating from the position of the criminals that might be brought before Schmidt. A third story, JB Jackson's "Interrogation of Der Schleim," concerns the interrogation of a hunchback and moves toward a place of surprising revelation.

Other stories here take some feeling or aspect or chance mention in Schmidt's diary and run with it, with the connection to Schmidt's original text being largely metaphorical or coming down to a few words: Alexander Palacio's "Ingenue", for instance, which seems as much heir to William Sampson's brief but startling tale "A Woman Seldom Found" as it is to Schmidt. Or John Daker's "To See a Black

Devil," which takes a prisoner's curse on the judges who condemned him from the ninetieth entry in Schmidt's diary and moves it forward in time and into the hard-boiled genre.

None of these stories are quite like each other. Some embrace Schmidt and his time, some glance off him on their way elsewhere. Each makes available a slightly different way of looking at the original. Each story both confirms that there is nothing new under the sun and yet somehow still gives the impression that it could only be written by the person who wrote it.

So, read these stories, then go read Schmidt, then read these stories again. They will feel both the same and different from how they felt the first time.

—*Brian Evenson*

THIRTY-ONE BLOWS

Brian Renninger

The church bells were not yet ringing. Neither was there a visit from the emperor who, so far as anyone had heard, remained sitting like a toad on his throne in Prague with one eye looking toward the Turks and the other at Bohemia. Nor was the sky filled with falling stars and fighting angels as older residents of Nuremberg remembered from near a quarter century previous. And it certainly was not something more mundane like a visitation from traveling minstrels. The hangman in black strolled down the street toward the Raven's Stone.

In his wake, curious voices wafted from jetty to jetty out casement windows to follow him down the shadowed street. The Henker, Meister Schmidt. Why was he out so early on a Sunday morn? Why did his black attire seem more austere than that of the other residents of Nuremberg also dressed in black? Why was his pace so brisk? Why was he carrying his sword? No executions were planned before to-morrow. Why did he stop to make the sign of the cross at each of the three confessionals along the way? He was already forbidden the sacrament. Surely, such shows of piety were of no use?

They watched his retreating, stolid figure. His raven cloak, left to its own devices, spread in the wind. The chill air punctuated each step with a puff of dragon breath. Soon he was past the echoing halls of the Klarissenkloster with its doddering and stubborn nuns, past the stout bulk of the Woman's Tower, and out the gateway. Out of his sight, the old women, each up to scrub their stoop on a Sunday morning, made small groups to gabble out their questions. They had no answers, but they invented them, nonetheless. Going to meet his master the dancing imp? No. No, said Ingrid, trysting with The Lion, commandment of the town archers and Schmidt's assistant, her paramour up upon the parapet, had seen a werewolf out among the fields. The Meister was out to do battle with the forces of darkness. Do battle? Ach, no. It can't be! The Henker's face had been an emotionless mask as he passed – it betrayed nothing. But, in the end, their eldest, Sibylle, bent over her gnarled oaken cane, turned a rheumy eye to the Henker's back. "You are all wrong, it has to have something to do with his brother-in-law." Then one by one they went back to their brushes, cracked the skim of ice forming over the water, and went down onto their calloused knees as if in prayer.

The truth of it was Schmidt was thinking about eggs. He was worried. That morning, as he'd come down from his tower to the kitchen for breakfast, Maria turned to him with a cross expression. "Look at this, it's the fourth one this morning!" She shifted infant Jorg to her other hip to hold out a broken egg for him to examine. Peering down, inside among blood and slime sat a dead and rotting half-grown chick. The smell of sulfur struck his nose. It wasn't so unusual, cocks being crafty enough to occasionally get at the hens unobserved, however watchful the farmer. But, four in a row? She paused and unconsciously rubbed her belly. She hardly showed yet but, were the eggs bad luck? A sign?

She dumped the bad egg in a ceramic crock, reached into the basket and broke another. She let out a snort. "Again! I won't be buying from Gerstleg in future unless he refunds me. It's ridiculous. Go to him. Take his nose. He'll fear looking a fool without a nose when he sees you coming. Bring your pincers, the money will leap from his purse. It's what your father would have done." She cackled to herself knowing he'd do nothing of the sort. His father, Heinrich, now living in near retirement in Bamberg, also an executioner, had never been a bully. "They all hate us anyway. Might as well get something from it." An attitude profoundly counter to Schmidt's own.

Schmidt ate his eggs and bread quickly and with a preoccupied air. The three children at table a cacophony that swirled around him. Vitus, a little whirlwind not yet out of skirts, repeatedly ran into the table leg and ignored his food. Vitus's younger sister, Margaretha, toddled behind shrieking at the top of her lungs. Even little Jorg's gurgling while he suckled seemed overly loud. Up from the table with a start, upstairs to gather his sword, satchel, and certain items, then back down to give Maria a dutiful kiss on the cheek. "Don't be late for church. I have errands." With that he threw on his cloak and went out into the February breeze. The door banging behind him only partly concealed Maria's frustrated exclamation at his abrupt exit.

Now, outside the city wall, proving the speculators wrong, he passed the Raven's Stone and turned toward the river. The gallows timbers were empty. He'd not had an execution since last November, Anna Freyin who'd drowned her two-year old boy in the well by the Franciscan church. Beheaded with the sword. Her fingers were in his satchel.

The wan morning light made the frozen Pegnitz a black line dividing stark banks of snow. The bridge was already crowded with anglers, with their poles, hatchets, and baskets, hoping for a renke or carp for Lent. Schmidt continued past the bridge to walk the bank. The snow crunched under his step. The cold made the hairs of his nose sting. The air smelled of mold and dead leaves which was refreshing after the wood smoke of the city. He saw his way, the path through the river willows. Like elfland, everyone knew this path but never tread it. Or, at least, never let their neighbors know they had.

Once within the willows Schmidt found himself in a place of shifting shadows and ice crystals striking rainbows from the rising sun. He thought of the story of Noah, and how the rainbow had brought hope. Perhaps this willow path led to hope as well? In the distance the church bells began to toll. Soon, through the leafless branches, he saw his destination. The hut built on a cart stood on a sandbar surrounded by reeds. One wheel of the cart leaned broken against a stump; the axle leveled by wooden blocks. The chimney puffed a thin white plume. Schmidt went up, knocked, and waited for an answer.

"M. are you there?"

A small portal in the door slid open. Light spilled into gray morning transfixing Schmidt in his place. A child's eye appeared in the opening—blue with curled blonde lock tumbling above it. "He is here. Have you brought what you promised?

Schmidt almost stammered but then paused and drew himself up. No need to fear a child, "Of course I have. I gave my word. Will M. keep his?"

The child giggled a high-pitched peal. "He will. Your brother-in-law cannot be saved from death tomorrow. But his soul can be saved from the flames."

"That is all I ask. I will do what's needed."

Schmidt brought from his satchel the small parcel containing Anna Freyin's fingers. The eye disappeared from the portal and a hand reached out. The hand was an unholy amalgamation of raptor's claw and a human hand. Dirty yellow nails and scaled skin. Schmidt stepped back startled, blinked, and the gnarled talon was gone. He could see a child's hand, small and pink and clean. "Cross my palm."

Schmidt did so and the hand withdrew to be replaced by the eye again. "But more is needed if this is to be done."

"More? The fingers were all M. asked for!"

"Oh, the fingers are necessary but insufficient. It takes much more to pull a man's soul from the pit. Especially an unrepentant man's soul. Follow the river downstream until you come upon a blue barn with a missing roof. Talk to the farmer there. Carry out his errand. Bring me the head."

"The head?"

"You will know it. When you bring the head, the essential salts will have been prepared. Hold forth your sword."

Schmidt drew his sword and held it up to the opening. The child's fingers snapped out and grasped the blade hard, drawing blood. Yet, it was not blood. At first dark red, it soon swirled with silver. The smell of rotten eggs struck Schmidt's nose just as he'd smelled at breakfast earlier. Absurdly, his stomach gurgled as if he were hungry. The liquid flowed down the fuller of his sword, glowing red and silver like a mixture of molten sulfur and hydrargyrum. The fluid beaded and settled into the words engraved on the blade. The words dissolved and shifted and reformed and settled into a new configuration. Soon, the liquid was gone, absorbed into the metal of the blade itself.

The hand withdrew. The portal snapped shut.

Schmidt was left standing stunned in the stillness of morning. All was quiet within the hut. Even the chimney stood cold. He leaned forward to peer at the blade. The sword was a gift from his father, given after completing his apprenticeship. His father had had it inscribed, as the Puritan had requested, with Psalm 23:4. Schmidt had often wondered, especially after putting a man to the question, whether the rod and staff did comfort the sinner? But now, now the words had changed. The inscription now read, "Es ist nicht tot, was ewig schlafen kann. Und in seltsamen Äonen sogar der Tod kann sterben." He sheathed his tool in wonder.

Schmidt was befuddled. What could it mean, "…even death can die"? Nothing could be made of it. He sucked ice crystals from his mustache and stolidly moved to sit on a log at the edge of the ice. From his satchel he withdrew a pair of skates and began strapping them on.

Before long Schmidt was gliding down the ice of the frozen Pegnitz. He moved with speed on the steel blades. For the first time this morning he felt alive and free. The farms were somber on either side of the frozen flow. As he exerted himself the sun came to shine down the length of the river causing it to blaze orange and gold like a copper viper moving sinuously through the still countryside. But it was he, Schmidt, not the river that was moving. Blood surged through his body. His heart pounded in his temples. His chest spewed forth great gouts of dragon breath causing his whiskers to grow icicles. Despite the urgency of his task, he sometimes was compelled swoop in great circles and arcs. On the ice he almost forgot about his job on the morrow.

All too soon he saw the barn with no roof. His joy was done. The thatch scattered in the snow. The blue-washed walls now crudely painted with the image of a red hen. He knew immediately what had gone on. *Mörderbrenners*, murder-burners. He was not wrong. Talking with the farmer, Grüble by name, a squat, aging, avuncular man seeming to have risen from the very soil itself, he learned that soldiers had come the night before. Or, rather, unemployed *landsknecht* turned bandits. They'd come with promises to burn both his barn and his house. They stole the timbers and his milk cow and left with threats to return with torches unless he could come up with more for them. Was there anything the good Meister could do? Schmidt sucked ice from his mustache and said, "We shall see. We shall see." He bade the man goodbye to trudge in the direction pointed out by the farmer, his equally squat wife, and three children.

As he labored, Schmidt knew this farmer, this man, his wife, his children. The folk of Nuremburg arose and went home well-fed to their houses protected by walls and archers—fearing nothing but wars and the rarity of plague. But Schmidt had known farmers as a boy in the little town of Hof. Farmers had no need of wars or rare perils. The eternal war was with hunger. A drought or hard winter were to them pitched battles. Now for this farmer it was as if the wolves had entered a sheepfold. The loss of his barn like the loss of a fortress.

He thought of the Puritan. The Puritan had come visit Hof when his father was beginning Schmidt's apprenticeship. The man was English and, given to wandering, had found himself some adventures in the Black Forest. Afterwards, he'd come to Hof to rest after his unnamed exertions and taken up with Heinrich despite (or perhaps because of) their family's dishonor. The Puritan, with his gimlet eye and horse face, would watch Frantz behead dogs at his father's command. Upon seeing Frantz flinch he'd said in his poor German, "All these strays have been taken up as biters, chicken raiders, thieves. Remember, they are guilty, Frantz. Mercy to the guilty is cruelty to the innocent." Schmidt took these words to heart. The words had served him well. Though, while the Puritan had a burning passion for justice, the Puritan had less an interest in law. Perhaps it was an English trait? In any case, Schmidt had always been content to let guilt be determined by those in authority. His current mission haunted him. Determining guilt was not his role. He was no judge. He was only an executioner.

At length he stood before a black wood. The tracks he'd followed were unmistakable. A large band of men had dragged heavy timbers through the snow into the forest. Schmidt was at a loss. He was no warrior. He bore a sword, but he was no swordsman. In any case his tool was no weapon of war: no point, too heavy. A cleaver. An instrument of death, yes, but not an instrument for fighting. It was neither handy nor nimble. Nonetheless, he would see this through. Schmidt stalked into the gloom of the forest.

In the forest, he found them. The soldiers, dressed in colors and slashes, and mixed finery against every sumptuary commandment. Yet, the fine clothing was blood-stained, and mud-stained, and torn. The company lounged around a bonfire, the farmer's timbers keeping Old Man Winter's cold at bay. Nearby, a pile of the farmer's remaining timbers with the soldier's pikes and large swords stacked against it. One motley fellow milked the cow into a steaming bucket.

Schmidt stepped into the clearing with bared sword. He stood there, sword held downward, the tip in the snow. At first, they didn't see him. Then one looked up to see another among them. The man nudged his neighbor who looked up and nudged another. And so, it went around the fire until every eye had turned toward Schmidt. The man at the cow missed the bucket to send a stream into the snow.

"Do you know me?" asked Schmidt.

The largest amongst the soldiers stepped forward. He was a monster of a man: tall, well-muscled, with angry black eyes. Hair stood out from under his cap, his large fore-arms matted with hair, hair peeked from the laced neck of his doublet, hair from his smashed nose blended with the hair of his mustache.

"Ya, I know you. You are the Henker—Schmidt."

"Meister Schmidt."

"Are you here to join us at the fire, Hencker? Tired of torturing whores and flogging thieves out of town? Well, we are a hospitable people. Take a seat."

"No. You are to return farmer Grüble's cow and timbers."

"They are burning already. Besides, we would be cold and hungry." The large soldier turned and sauntered over to the weapons. He picked up a beast of a sword with both hands. Turning to Schmidt, the soldier swung it like a child swings a willow wand to knock down blades of grass. It was impressive to move such a large weapon so easily. In his hands, the sword seemed more a toy than a weapon.

"If you know me, soldier, then you know I am no warrior," said Schmidt.

"Then you are a fool to come here with a sword, Henker. Go back to town. There is no law here."

"Return the timbers and cow. Go to Cologne. Ernst von Bayern is hiring soldiers."

"I don't think we shall. Farmer Grüble is still too good a host. Join us at the fire. Help us eat Grüble's cow. Or head back to the town you are better suited for."

"I made a promise."

"A promise to whom, Hencker? To your master Mephistopheles?" At this the men at the fire gave a round of chuckling laughter.

Schmidt stood silent.

The soldier attacked. While Schmidt expected such, nevertheless, the strike nearly took him unawares. Two steps and he came within measure. The huge sword swinging toward Schmidt. Only through luck was Schmidt able to interpose his own sword between himself and the gargantuan blade. It was a miracle. The two blades touched, and the soldier's sword shivered into a hundred pieces to leave the soldier holding nothing but the hilt and a stump of the blade. The large man fell back with a shriek. Shards of metal were embedded in his hands and cheeks. The inscription on Schmidt's blade burned like heated copper. Schmidt stood dumbfounded.

"Ach! I see you have indeed consorted with the Devil! You are not alone! The farmer is no innocent. Did you not see his prosperity? So far from any town? M. brings us riches each to our own nature."

"Lie all you like. Return the timbers and the cow."

Silhouetted against the fire the soldier was nothing but a black shape. Then the shape changed. The man turned his head up to howl. It seemed to Schmidt that the soldier's smashed nose now was more of a muzzle. From the lungs of a man came the howl of a wolf. The soldier crouched low and flexed. The shreds of his doublet, hose, and boots fell free. What stood before Schmidt now had eyes glowing orange, claws where once were fingers, and the already hairy form now stood in bristling fur. A line of drool dropped from slavering fangs to run down distended jaws and into the snow.

The man, now a beast, came at Schmidt on all four legs. It bounded through the snow, its claws tearing up black clods of earth. It came at Schmidt all fangs, fur, lolling tongue, fire, and fury. As it came it roared.

Schmidt closed his eyes and held his sword out before him. The monster came on obliviously and leaped. Even with no point, Schmidt's sword entered the beast like a hot poker through grease. Schmidt was bowled over. The stench of the beast's breath engulfed him and then was gone. The sword tore from his grasp as the wolf-thing went past him to fall thrashing in the snow. The beast flailed and howled, "Betrayed!" The human voice shockingly horrific coming from such a throat. The writhing seemed to go on for a long time. Then the creature fell still amid a growing red rose staining the snow. The men at the fire stood silent in shock.

Schmidt picked himself up, calmly walked over to the corpse and withdrew the sword. Then, with an expert strike beheaded the creature with a single stroke. Schmidt found himself relieved not to have botched the blow. He may be no warrior, but he had pride of profession. The head now removed; the body became that of a man. Yet, the head remained that of a wolf. Schmidt grabbed a fistful of coarse bristles and hoisted the gruesome trophy up over his shoulder. He turned back toward the fire.

"Return the cow and what timbers remain. Head to Cologne. I hear Ernst von Bayern has need of soldiers. Stay here or trouble farmer Grüble more and I shall see you all broken by the wheel." Dragging his sword behind him, Schmidt made toward the black wood.

A voice called out, "But, Meister Schmidt, if we return the cow what will we eat?"

Schmidt stopped, turned back toward the men to fix them with his eyes. He pointedly looked down at the already stiffening corpse, "I've left you meat. What more do you want?"

He turned his back to the appalled soldiers and stalked into the wood. It was as if he were a phantom. The men began to gather up the remaining timbers.

It was well after dark when he approached the city gates with his cloak, like bat wings, wrapped about him against the cold. The archers were reciting poems of love to each other to keep the cold and sleep at bay.

"…By what witchcraft wert thou made,
Thou empty cause of solid harms
But I shall find out countercharms,
Thy airy devilship to remove
From this circle here of love."
Schmidt thumped the sallyport with the hilt of his sword.

"Go away! The gates don't open until morning," shouted the archer keeping watch above.

"You'll open for me! It is I, Meister Schmidt. Open or I'll have The Lion after you."

And so, with grumbles of "why didn't you say so" and "no need to get snitty" was the portal opened to let the weary Henker back into the town of Nuremberg. The streets were pitch but Schmidt could navigate by the few candles burning in windows and the sounds of the river. Not a body did he see about. Every soul had no desire to be out in the frigid dark. At length he was crossing the Hangman's Bridge to see his own candle shining in the window of home.

Schmidt let himself in to find himself greeted by Vitus and Margaretha at the head of the stair. "Oho!" he whispered. "What are you two doing out of bed? You'll catch your death."

The two tumbled down the stairs into Schmidt's arms. "We were waiting for you. You were gone so long."

"Well, I'm back now, you two ragamuffins. Let's get you into bed." He hauled them upstairs to dump them onto their pallet, pack them tight in quilts, and tweak their noses. They were asleep before he left the room.

Maria was snoring when he stepped softly into their room. The baby, Jorg, silent in his truckle. His sword and satchel went into the corner. He donned his sleeping gown and cap. Then he lifted the covers to climb into the bed. He was careful not to disturb the pan of coals Maria had brought to bed with her. He fell, exhausted, to sleep.

Sleep did not last. He lay, listening to Maria's soft snoring. He thought about his day. The business of the fingers. The fight. The overjoyed farmer. He'd divested himself of the werewolf's head at M.'s hut and taken up the pouch of Anna Freyin's fingers, now reduced to essential salts. The hut had been silent upon his return but the pouch hung by a nail. He left the wolf head propped on the broken wagon wheel. Tomorrow would be a trying day, what with the execution to come.

He supposed it reflected poorly upon him to have to execute his brother-in-law. For, while the trial was yet to be completed, the outcome was foreordained. The confessions had been made. Schmidt hadn't had to work long with the strappado and small stone before the truth sprang forth like starlings startled from their nest. It enraged him. That his sister married such an infamous character as Potter Freddy was beyond him. Well, really, it wasn't, she was already widowed once, and their shared family dishonor made more suitable matches quite unlikely. Nonetheless. She had begged Schmidt to save him. Such is the love of a woman.

What of the love of the townspeople? The townspeople, always gossiping about him—speculating on this and that. He was a minion of the Devil. He performed black magic. His children were imps and homunculi. His wife a whore with himself a hypocrite who branded whores and flogged them out of town. It mattered not to them how many legs of theirs he set, or wounds stitched up. He'd always be without honor.

If only his father, Heinrich, hadn't been bullied by the Bellator into being his executioner, forever dooming his lineage. A dishonor only increased by the events of the day. The deals made. The tasks carried out. Maria must never know. She'd have his blood otherwise. He loved her but he was also wary. She could be passionate and uncharitable. After all, she was the daughter of a warehouse laborer and thus not raised in refinement. As if he himself, Schmidt, was refined. He was a village yokel with dreams of being accepted in the city. Schmidt slept a fitful sleep, his worries turning his dreams into a rough and tumble battle between pygmies and cranes among the clouds.

Schmidt woke well before sunrise with Maria still snoring at his side, blood and feathers roiling inside his head. The day must begin. He slowly left the bed, gathered yesterday's soiled clothes, and went downstairs to try to brush the mud out from his clothing as best he could. He couldn't look ragged as he had duties to attend to. For this day especially he needed to present himself well. It was but a year before Vitus's birth the city fathers had appointed him as Henker. He had finished his probation, but the town had yet to fully know him. He had to be without stain.

Schmidt hadn't worked long when Maria came down with the infant on her breast. It was not long before she had the stove melting the iced windows. Quicker than he thought possible she brought him a stein of hot ale and a bowl of broth to drink. She knew he liked to take a light breakfast on working days. Taking the brush and doublet from him she said, "Give me that. I prepared a fresh ruff for you last night."

Maria disappeared to practice secret womanly arts leaving Schmidt to sip his broth in silence. He watched the ice melt on the windows. The frost sublimed from the top down leaving an inverted arc of slowly diminishing ice in each pane. Soon his mind had vanished into the ice thinking of the arcs his skates had made in the river, the arcs in the oxbows of the Pegnitz, the arc of a sword, the arc of a severed head falling, the arc of a spray of blood, the arc of a life.

"Father, we had dreams!" Startled from his reverie, Schmidt looked up. It was little Vitus and peering from behind him even smaller Margaretha. Schmidt set down his bowl and wiped his mustaches. "Climb into my lap and tell me all about them!" Vitus swarmed up his legs. He had to bend to lift Margaretha up.

"It was a nightmare!" said Vitus. "An incubus!" said Margaretha.

"I was chased by hound. Or a wolf!" said Vitus. "I swam in a lake of fire! Or maybe it was a river," said Margaretha. Margaretha burst into tears. "Oh, I cannot swim, Father! I sank into the waters. I know not the colors but there were flames."

Schmidt hugged and jostled the two. "Now, now, they are but dreams. You stayed up too late waiting for me last night. Sip some of my broth. It will calm your minds." Dutifully, the two had their sips just as Maria burst back into the room. "You two! Up already! Leave your father be, he has work today." She began hanging his, now cleaned, clothes by the stove to dry.

"Can we come watch you work today father?" It was Vitus's common refrain.

"No, you may not! You are both too young," said Maria.

"Vitus, when your head reaches the top of this table you may come and watch. Soon after that we'll begin your practice with the sword."

"Enough with such talk," said Maria. "Frantz, go use the privy and clean your teeth. Your clothes will be dry by then." Nine years his senior, Maria often took a tone of a mother to him. She had come to the marriage with no dowry from a family of seven children, she'd spent most of her life tending to her brothers and sisters and, by the time Frantz had met her, her habits of speech were ingrained beyond Schmidt's ability to correct.

So up the tower he went to perform his ablutions. Then back downstairs for his clothes, followed by a dash back up to dress. After dressing he donned his satchel, checking to ensure the pouch of salts was still ensconced within. Checking the blade of the sword, he saw with some relief that the engraving had returned to the Psalm. The magic was gone. Maria sometimes sharpened the blade and he had been dreading questions. He would not be using the sword this day, but the blade was something of a badge of office. Plus, if the town fathers did indulge him, it would be best not to have to dash home to retrieve the tool. He left his cloak behind. He'd have to suffer the cold so as not risk losing face entangled at crucial moments in his duty. So equipped, he headed to the door.

"Wait!" said Maria. She rushed over to peck his cheek and straighten his ruff. This gave Vitus and Margaretha time to latch upon each leg. "Don't go father! Stay home! Play with us!"

Maria levered the children free. Behind her, baby Jorg started to cry, upset by the tumult. As he wedged himself out the cracked door Maria whispered in his ear, "Do us proud today. Make Friedrich hurt. Do your duty. Oh!" She grabbed Schmidt's hand and pressed it into her belly. Then came a tiny kick, barely perceptible. Life proceeded onward. Schmidt tumbled out into cold morning air like a clockwork man springing from a box.

Schmidt passed over the covered bridge that fed into the Water Tower asylum, grunted at the warden, and went right out the corner door into the crystal morning light. Quickly down the cobbled streets, treading carefully to avoid the icy patches. It would not do for the townspeople to see him go sprawling. Then he was in the Main Market, the smells of the nearby pig market and the slaughterhouses over the river nearly masked by savory odors of roasting sausages and boiling kraut.

He found Gerstleg huddled among his caged chickens wearing a massive woolen cap and engulfed in a thick brown blanket littered with down and bloom. Gerstleg's face was obscured by his muttering breath. The only visible portion of his flesh visible were wizened hands endlessly working the beads of a plain wooden paternoster hanging in a loop from his belt. Schmidt did not promise to take his nose or any other threat. Schmidt instead whispered an order and proffered a coin. Gerstleg soon produced a string-tied bundle of eggs.

Having obtained the eggs, Schmidt headed north to the Town Hall and the Hole. Schmidt banged into Friedrich Werner's cell with the meal. "Up you get Potter Freddy! Rise and shine!" Freddy didn't move. He lay on the slab shivering, wrapped in a coarse blanket. Schmidt set the plate and tankard down on the slab. Grasping the blanket, he tumbled Freddy to the floor.

Freddy heaved himself up and sat. He took the plate and ate a sausage. "Wait a little while, Frantz. Let me eat." His arms were weak from the strappado. The muscles around his shoulders were bruised bright blue, the color of a bird's egg.

"Call me Meister Schmidt. Put your shirt on, Freddy, we need you ready for your sentencing."

"I'm to have a measure of wine with my meal." Even in his current state, unshaven and crippled by the strappado, Freddy was a handsome man. Schmidt could see what his sister saw in him. He was well built, with a strong chin, fine hair, and a turned-up mustache now a little worse for the wear. Frantz slapped him across the back of his head. The plate went flying to scatter sausages across the floor.

"Have my friends come? Another day, perhaps, they are riding many a mile." Freddy began gathering the sausages.

"Have you a fever? Hertal isn't coming. I took his head last July, remember?"

"I have other friends, but, yes, I remember. For what we did to your sister."

"You made her happy once. She asked that I spare you, as if it were up to me. What did you get? A little silver? A little gold? You left her for dead in the Schwabach. She survived."

"Oh, yes, you have a fine sister!" Suddenly Freddy was animated. "She warmed my blood from cold. It didn't last, nor did her money." Freddy gnawed a now-cold sausage and abruptly sunk again into a funk. "My friends will come to vouch for me, just one more day." He grabbed the tankard to gulp the ale greedily.

"You have no friends. Everything has but one end, Freddy, only a sausage has two. Today is the day."

In due course, they stood before the Town Fathers for the sentencing, along with Freddy's stepfather and sister. "For the crimes of shooting dead your travelling companion at Buch, killing and robbing a man in the Erlangen wood, and, thirdly murdering a boy in the Fischbach wood with a stone, leaving the boy to die in the hospital, not to mention assisting in the assault and near murder of your wife in Swabia and a dozen robberies, you are hereby sentenced to six nips, with glowing tongs, two in front of the town hall, two in front of Saint Lorenz Church and two by Saint Martha's by the gate. To be followed by execution by the wheel. Has anyone anything to say for this poor sinner?"

Freddy's stepfather and sister did have things to say, namely requests for leniency and mercy which fell upon deaf ears though the rejection was given gently. As expected, Schmidt would not be using the sword today. "Schmidt, you look like you have something to say. What is it?"

Schmidt cleared his throat. He didn't care for public speaking. "Ahem, it's just this, sirs. Might we reduce the nips? Be a shame to spare him the wheel. I don't reckon he will survive more than two."

The town fathers conferred in whispers, then, "Very well, in deference to your judgement and relation, nips are reduced to two, to be administered in the tumbrel on the way to the Raven Stone." The head of the Blood Court pierced Schmidt with a keen eye. "So long as you agree to make him a horrifying example. Do you understand?"

"Understood, sirs."

"So be it. Which being against the laws of the Holy Roman Empire, my Lords have decreed and given sentence that he shall be condemned from life to death by two nips of the red-hot tongs and by the wheel." The judge then polled each member of the court, who responded with the ritual, "What is legal and just pleases me."

"Executioner, I command you in the name of the Holy Roman Empire, that you carry out the aforesaid punishment." The white staff smote the floor.

Then out of the Town Hall and into the tumbrel waiting outside. The Blood Court in red and black robes proceeded Schmidt, followed by the town Chaplain, then Schmidt and Freddy, behind the town fathers in black finery marching in rows. Augustin Amman, Schmidt's assistant, The Lion, had prepared everything. He'd cleaned the cart, normally used to carry manure and other waste to dump into the Pegnitz, and set up the brazier, gloves, bellows, and tongs, in one corner; in another corner leaned the hammer, stakes, lath, cord, and wheel. The sentence was anticipated.

Indeed, a crowd had already gathered. The route to the Raven's Stone was lined with spectators. A few dozen of The Lion's archers, in steel caps and cuirass, armed with halberds, kept the crowd at a distance from the cart.

Vendors carrying plates and baskets hawked sausages, salt herring, and sweets. As usual, a carnival atmosphere prevailed. Frost from the massed breath coalesced into clouds above the throng, mixing with the woodsmoke of the city. Children bundled into vaguely human shapes tossed snowballs. The older children pulled their younger siblings on sleds.

Amman looped Freddy's bonds on the hooks for that purpose. Then he whipped the horse into motion. The tumbrel moved toward the Raven's Stone. The sword went into the corner with the wheel. Schmidt donned the gloves, inspected the cooling coals in the brazier, gathered the bellows and pumped life back into the embers. A cloud of sparks swirled into the sky drawing forth an exclamation from the crowd. The tongs were not yet white hot but only a dull cherry. "Take it easy on the speed, Amman."

"Yes, sir. Also, now might be the time for the wine." He produced a tankard.

Schmidt took the container and flipped the cap to pour the small package of salts into the vessel. The powder swirled for a moment in the dark liquid and then was gone. He lifted Freddy's chin to look him in the eye. "You don't deserve it, but my sister asked for me to show you mercy. Drink this, it will help."

Greedily Freddy did so. "It tastes strange."

"The medicine, Freddy, it takes some time to work, you'll feel the tongs but by the time we reach the Raven's Stone you'll feel nothing. You'll be spared the pain of the wheel."

Schmidt worked the bellows, then held the instrument up for the crowd to see. The pincers of the tongs glowed white hot. He placed the tongs back into the coals. He pulled Freddy's shirt down to hang at his waist.

"Ready, Freddy?" Schmidt pulled the tongs from the coals and whipped them in the air. Again, the crowd let out a hoot. Schmidt brought the glowing pincers down to grasp the meat between Freddy's shoulder, armpit, and breast. The muscle was deep there. The glowing tongs sank into the flesh giving off a succulent roasting smell. A puff of vapor escaped into the cold air. Schmidt squeezed with all his strength. Freddy screamed and tried to writhe away from the hot metal. There was no retreat. Schmidt leaned implacably into the tongs. They cooled and cooked themselves into the flesh. Then, with a flourish, Schmidt tore the tongs free, drawing another agonizing shriek from his victim. The crowd roared with delight. Women and children pointed. Men joked and slapped each other on the back. Freddy slumped forward, whimpering.

"That's one, Freddy. Thank me that I talked them down to two." The cart proceeded forward as Schmidt placed the tongs back into the coals and worked the bellows.

This time the nip was over Freddy's left kidney. Freddy didn't scream but a trickle of blood leaked from his lips where he'd bit his tongue. He sank against his bonds and lost control of his bladder. The ammoniac stink was crisp in the air. The crowd roared.

"I think it's starting to work, Henker. It's strange. Maria is speaking. Vitus wants to come watch. Maria says 'no'." Freddy looked about in panic.

"Keep my family's names off your lips, Freddy. Wait, the effect will increase. That's the two. Enjoy your time before the Raven's Stone."

Schmidt relaxed, too. Working in a moving tumbrel was difficult. He was glad this part was over and braced himself for the next operation. The wheel was the most difficult of his duties. The crowd followed like sheep following their shepherd's bell. Sensing the lull, the hawkers again raised their voices. Citizens bought treats and then jogged to catch up.

As they approached the Woman's Tower and gate, Schmidt caught sight of a face in a window of the Klarissenkloster. Unmoving, the white of her wimple standing out from the interior gloom, the face was old, unsmiling and judgmental. A stern nun of Saint Clare, forever looking out at the world that had left her behind and, as always, finding the world wanting.

There was a momentary pileup as the procession passed through the gate. The crowd spilled out the gate like water pouring forth from a newly opened floodgate. Outside the walls, the Raven's Stone stood with its gibbets and scaffolds. The platform was a little worse for wear but still had plenty of life left in it. Soon after being hired by the city, Schmidt had the original Raven's Stone replaced. The decayed structure wasn't safe to work on. He'd torn the structure down himself and had the town fathers order all the men of the guilds to construct a new one. Thereby the dishonor of the structure spread equally among the townspeople. By this means, no one could be shunned. Except for Schmidt, of course.

Only two bodies hung from the scaffolds: that of Anna Freyin, the salts of her fingers Freddy had drunk; and Michael Mülner, horse thief. Freyin was near entirely bones now but the approaching procession sent a few ravens and crows into the blue sky. A second crowd was already surrounding the platform having chosen to forego the delights of the nips in favor of claiming front row views of the wheel. All the worst hussars, dressed in their best red and white, were elbowing aside the townspeople, staking out the best views with shaken fists and ejaculations in Polish and broken German. The company would soon head north to the growing war over the Diocese of Cologne. Finding employment, Schmidt guessed more than half the horsemen would be dead by this time next year. Let them have some entertainment, he supposed.

Schmidt displayed Freddy on the stairs while Amman made the preparations. The crowd fell silent. The Chaplain asked, "Have you any words of contrition?" There was one last chance to save his soul. Schmidt knew there was yet another. "Speak," said Schmidt, "confess all and I will help you get through this as quickly as possible."

"Amman, prepare the stakes and the laths."

For a moment all that was heard were the calls of the birds and the rhythmic blows of Amman's hammer pounding in the stakes like the sounding of a metronome counting out the last measures of a requiem. Freddy leaned forward to whisper in the ear of the Chaplain. No one could understand what he said. The hussars started shouting, "Speak to us all, jailbird! Tell us your deeds!" The hammer continued pounding. Freddy startled away from the Chaplain and looked around as if surprised. "Tell my friend Hertal he was too late to save me. I forgive him." Then Freddy became lucid and grinned. "Remember me to the daughter of butcher Wolf Kleinlein. I forget her name, but I shall remember her in the afterlife. I expect many others shall as well." The hussars guffawed and made rude hand gestures. Amman's hammer stopped.

Schmidt would be under suspicion if death came early. All must be done with attention to detail. Freddy seemed back in a daze as Schmidt made his arms and feet fast to the stakes and propped the lath under each bone of his arms and legs. Schmidt circled Freddy testing the bonds. It would not do for the cords to break partway through. Death by the wheel was rare. Schmidt had performed the ritual only a handful of times since completing his apprenticeship. Best to do it well.

Schmidt heaved up the wheel. It was heavy. Lifting it strained the muscles of his back. Holding the device above his head he turned a full circle so all could see it. As a demonstration of its soundness, he broke a spare length of lath. The crack of the wood sent a murmur through the onlookers. He tossed the fragments to the crowd. Children scrambled to obtain the souvenirs. Now it was time. He raised the wheel up and set to work. There came a crash and a scream.

At length the broken corpse stood before him. Thirty-one blows in all. Sometimes, as a favor, the killing blow to the throat was carried out before attention was paid to the limbs. Not this day. Broken bone stood out white from the flesh and blood. The hussars guffawed and pointed, "See, he's dressed as us now. Red and white." As intended, the death was not an easy one. Amman revived Freddy with smelling salts each time he lost consciousness. While screams were normal, Freddy's cries had risen to an unusual pitch. The salts administered did nothing for the pain. This should have gladdened Schmidt. Mercy to the guilty is cruelty to the innocent.

Yet the screams troubled him. Especially those cries near the end. Freddy's last words were in a different voice, "Father! Father! What are you doing? No! Don't do this to me!" In the end he seemed more an animal than a person. Or a child. Who was Freddy addressing? God? Or, like most subjects of torture, the torturer? Schmidt was hardened to the usual cries. These words seemed personal.

The ritual was not yet done. Schmidt leaned the wheel against his body while Amman cut

Freddy's remains free. Schmidt tumbled the wheel flat on the surface of the Raven's Stone. Together, Schmidt and Amman took up the corpse to weave the shattered limbs into the spokes and lash them in place. Schmidt levered the wheel onto its rim and clumsily rolled it to the tripods. Freddy's head comically flopped about. Together they lifted the adorned wheel to fit its hub onto the tripod spike. The ritual complete, Freddy's corpse now stood for all to see above the Raven's Stone. Schmidt yanked a spoke to set the wheel spinning in a horrific unbalanced motion. With each rotation Schmidt could hear Freddy's teeth clack together. Life was hard; it was good to see how it could be harder.

Schmidt turned to the Blood Court. "Lord Judge, have I executed well?"

"You have executed as judgement and law have required."

"For that I thank God and my master who has taught me such art."

Already, the crowd was dispersing. The brief relief from their labors now over, the work of survival must begin anew. Schmidt left the cleanup to Amman. He made his way down the steps of the Raven's Stone into the thinning crowd. A few of the hussars slapped him on the back and forced a bottle of a strong liquor upon him. Schmidt swigged from the neck and choked. He'd rather have the refreshment of a beer. The field around the Raven's Stone was churned to black mud. He followed the arcs of the tumbrel's tracks back through the gate.

Freddy's final words preyed upon his mind as he slowly made his way back through the gate, along the city streets. "No, father! Don't do this to me!" What had Freddy meant by this? The condemned often raved at the end, mad with desperation. Perhaps there was nothing to make of it other than the words of madness? Schmidt shook his head in confusion. Had something gone wrong with M.'s salts?

The ice on the streets had long melted. The hangman's residence was on an island and considered separate from the city. He was lucky. Normally executioners were required to live outside a town's walls. He felt lighter now. The duty done. He hadn't shamed himself in front of the town fathers nor the spectators. The shade of the tunnel of the Hangman's Bridge chilled him as he crossed the river. At the far end of the bridge the shutters of his home shone in the bright afternoon sun like blood and bone.

From the bridge, he saw the faces of Vitus and Margaretha peering from a window in the tower. Seeing him, the faces disappeared. "I'm home. I've brought fresh eggs!" There was the patter of small feet running down the stairs.

Maria got to him first. She hugged him and said, "Feel the kicks. The little one has been kicking up a storm for the last half hour or more." Then Maria's brow furrowed. "Oof, that one hurt a little. How was the execution?"

"The baby's strong. That is good," said Schmidt. The boy and the girl joined them, chortling to see their father. Margaretha was clumsily dragging infant Jorg in his basket. Jorg, unhappy with such a rough journey, bawled. Maria and Schmidt held each other amid laughter and tears.

He awoke still exhausted, his mind filled with images of swimming in a pool of fire. He'd paddled endlessly away from flames of unknown color. Schmidt rested throughout the day and played with Vitus and Margaretha. Vitus stated he wanted to be a soldier and wear a tall hat. Margaretha stated solemnly that she'd like a fine dress for her birthday. Maria complained all day of the kicks from the growing baby, her brow growing more furrowed and pained as the day wore on.

The following day Schmidt must work. Three thieves to be hanged in Hersbruck. Schmidt rose well before the light and was out of the city before any of the gossips were up. Skating rather than taking the road. The rising sun found Schmidt winging his way in arcs and circles down the Pegnitz. He was free and happy. He loved the flutter of his cloak behind him. He was entranced with the illusion of being still as the glowing countryside moved past him. He elaborately doffed his cap and bowed while sliding backwards past M.'s hut. The small puff of the chimney seemed a cheerful signal this day. He waved as he passed stocky Grüble—up a ladder, repairing the thatch on his barn. He was exhausted yet mentally aflame by the time he made Hersbruck.

The town was tiny but well-to-do being situated on the Golden Road all travelers must pass between Nuremberg and Prague. Hersbruck was famous for being the birthplace of a prominent composer, now residing in Dresden, whose hymns a band played by portable organ as Schmidt hoisted the three criminals high on the gibbets. The bodies jerked in time to the music. Schmidt gave each rascal a good tug by the feet, and he was finished before the midday meal was done. He was back on the ice and made Nuremberg by midnight. Following the usual argument and grousing by the archers, Schmidt walked the streets home under the light of dancing aurora. Behind him, the archer's voices resumed their declaiming poetry.

"They are sweeter
And more precious
After the pains,
O God of Love,
The joys that you give.
Such that from your Divinity
If the joys,
Would not be given with the pain
No one would worship you."

Maria met him at the door, "The little one is still kicking." She was an experienced mother with three births under her belt. None of her other pregnancies had been like this. So much movement by the babe. Schmidt brewed Maria a hot tea and sent her to bed. But he was worried too. Perhaps, M. had scamped the rite?

The following week he hanged Cavalier Johnny, a card sharp and bigamist who, as his last words sang two songs: "When My Hour Is at Hand" and "Whatever God Wills." Schmidt allowed the three wronged woman, each big in belly, to tug Johnny's feet as a favor. When asked for any words of contrition for the court, Johnny cursed the jurors and, Schmidt felt, himself. "God guard you. For treating me this way may you one day see a black devil." The words shook Schmidt. His mind danced with visions of a lake of unknown fire. He suspected what pursued him was, in fact, the Devil. Freddy's last cries haunted him. "No, father! Don't do this to me!"

Weeks passed. Work was monotonous: a whore flogged out of town with rods; a thief flogged out of town with rods; a lewd couple, both married to other people, flogged out of town with rods; and a bigamist flogged out of town with rods. Maria continued to complain of kicks and pains. Indeed, she complained of more than kicks, she felt the little jaws working, gnawing. Maria took to her bed, to lay wincing every few minutes. The family became haggard. His Lion, Amman, took notice and began to take on more and more of Schmidt's duties. Vitus and Margaretha became quiet and morose. Jorg refused to suckle. The children rarely played, choosing instead to huddle in bed with their mother. Easter approached.

Every year in her time spring arced up from the flowery lands, causing the daffodils to bloom along the green way to the greater joys of the greening woods outside the city. The walls of the city shone white in the spring glare. The citizens of Nuremberg burst forth for picnics on the sward. Yet, within the City of Nuremberg all Schmidt and his family felt were unease, despair, fear, and pain. Neither the hidden glen, nor the blooming anemone on the sward, nor the joys of the shadowed woods were for them. The arc of spring had passed them by. Their arc proceeded in an entirely different direction.

The day before Easter Maria began screaming. "Look at it! Look at it!" Vitus and Margaretha scattered in terror. Jorg squalled in his truckle. Maria flung away the filthy bed clothes. "Do you see it, Frantz?" She pulled up her shift, exposing her growing belly. Stretch marks marred the flesh. She grabbed Schmidt's hand. "Feel!" Schmidt did so. Under the distended skin, it seemed he felt the head of the baby pressing soundly up from Maria's middle. He pulled his hand away and he saw the head clearly outlined against Maria's flesh. "Did you feel them? Frantz, do you see? The horns?"

"My god!" said Schmidt. He did see. Oh, how he saw. Maria swooned. Schmidt caromed out of the house to beg Amman to watch over the children. He left his confused Lion uncomfortably trying to console the children as if they were archers under his command. Again, the bad man in black drew the attention of the townspeople. He carried his sword over his shoulder and in the other hand, his skates clashing at his side.

There was no wind. His cloak did not stand out like bat wings. The cloak stood impotently like a man two days hanged. He did not stop at the confessionals. He was cursed. The women did not gossip but followed him silently with their eyes. Even old Sibylle had nothing to say. All had heard the troubles of his wife. All knew Schmidt's concerns even if they did not know where he was going. And Schmidt? Schmidt was thinking about what he saw pressed up against his wife's belly. The horns, yes. He had seen the horns. Worse, he'd glimpsed the features of the child within. To his mind, the features Schmidt saw were those of Potter Freddy.

Outside the wall, Schmidt took to the river path. He could not find the trail through the willows. He had lost it. The melting snows and budding trees concealed the entrance through the willows. Young daffodil buds stood up from the thawing snow. Flocks of birds were chanting to the Spring. He hacked at the willow branches with his sword, sending the birds scattering in all directions. Surely, M.'s hut had to be here somewhere?

Schmidt donned his skates. M.'s hut was obvious from the ice. Green shown poking up through the snow on the banks of the river. The effulgent sun blinded him. The river took on the copper look flowing away under the blades of his skates. Schmidt held a hand up against the dazzling heavens. The light pained his eyes so. Schmidt was a creature of darkness. Nowhere was M.'s hut visible.

Back and forth Schmidt hunted along the riverbank, finding nothing. If he could find

M., he could make the sorcerer turn back his spells. He would change M.'s mind. Recant their arrangement. Schmidt knew how to change people's minds. The rod, the staff, the stone, the wheel. If need be, he would seize M.'s child, the golden haired one, and turn his talents to the little one. Make the child bleed. He would bargain one child against another. Yet, as he skated, he saw nothing. No sandbar. No hut. Schmidt heard a giggle behind him like that of M.'s child. Schmidt dug his skates into a great arc heading towards the sound. Then he saw a great knot of toads. The beasts lined the bank in a great piled mass that thrashed and squirmed in the agonies of spring. He'd only heard their croaks.

Surely, Grüble's farm was just around the next bend? He had to have passed M.'s hut long ago. Gliding around the arc, Schmidt saw it. Not the hut. He saw the rubble of Grüble's farm. His skates clashed on rocks and sunk in mud as he headed to where the house and barn had stood. All was ashes. Kneeling among the debris he found the charred bones. Grüble, his wife, and children. The family had only temporarily been spared from the *Mörder-Brenners*.

He left the bones where they lay, turning back to river, to continue his forlorn quest. He must get back quickly. He was far, too far out of the way. M.'s hut was back the way he had come. His legs burned with the effort as he retreated upon the ice. Sweat dripped from his mustache both from the effort and the spring sun. He tasted salt, perhaps much like the taste of Anna Freyin's fingers. He did not swoop or loop in arcs. Only the fastest line would do.

Thinned by the spring sun, the ice gave way. With a crack like the breaking of a bone underneath the wheel, Schmidt disappeared under the ice. His skin burned with fire. All light was a smear of unknown colors. All was motion. The river flowed swiftly. The snake was now alive.

Schmidt rolled in the current. For a moment he lost all sense of up or down. Burning water choked him. He held desperately to his sword as he was borne downstream under the ice. Then his skates struck bottom. He was stabilized again but, with horror, realized he wasn't pushing against the bottom. He was inverted, skating against the underside of the ice with the current. He rolled. This time he found the bottom. He could push off the muck to bump roughly off the ice above. Schmidt choked on muddy river and pounded against the ice with the pommel of his sword.

Schmidt tumbled and stopped. He was against a submerged log. He pressed against the log, pushing his back against the ice. His skates skidded on the rotting wood. He gulped more water. The blades dug into the punk. He heaved. He inhaled water and thrashed. Fired burned his lungs. Once more he pushed. The ice gave way. He was through. Schmidt pulled himself onto the bank to gasp and choke out the icy fire into the warm spring air.

As he lay on the bank, Schmidt realized he heard a croaking. The rising and falling of the calls washed over him. Looking to the side he found himself under the gaze of the toads. Each amphibious face was turned toward him as if in judgement. As one, all the creatures fell silent while maintaining their unblinking stare. The females carried the males on their backs. One toad stood out, gazing at Schmidt with blue eyes. The blue eyes seemed less those of a toad than those of a bird—a raptor perhaps? Or a bird of paradise? Silently and in ranks, the writhing creatures turned their backs to hop up the riverbank into the black forest.

He did not find M.'s hut that day or any thereafter. It was as if the sandbar, the hut, the broken wheel, had never existed. The sun was a lake of fire on the horizon when he reached the gates of Nuremberg. He was soaked and mud covered with no hat when the prudently silent archers let him through. Schmidt's bedraggled visage and burning eyes gave the normally loquacious guards pause. No poetry followed at his heels.

Through the gate, and past the Woman's Tower, Schmidt trudged right through the corbelled arch that led to the doors of the Klarissenkloster. The nuns of Saint Clare had refused to abandon their faith and their property to the zealots of Martin Luther. They had made vows, they said—vows not to man but to God. The iconoclasts were transfixed by this moral rectitude. Hands that never hesitated to stick a dagger in a monk were stilled by the steely glares of the nuns. As their wombs did not swell in arcs, the nuns traveled in a straight line into the future.

Generations had passed, the nuns, in dwindling numbers true, persisted in their refutation of Martin Luther. Schmidt pounded on the doors with the pommel of his sword. There was no answer.

Schmidt continued. Light appeared in the door's small window. The door opened. Underlit by the taper in her hand, it was the nun he'd seen watching from the tumbrel. She just stood in the threshold saying nothing.

"A favor. I must speak with your leader!"

The nun said nothing.

"My spirit needs help. There is no one to whom I can turn."

The nun said nothing. The only sound was the hiss from her taper.

Schmidt dropped to his knees and pounded his head upon the ground. His sword lay abandoned. "Please. I have made a terrible mistake." His tears mixed with the mud of the courtyard. The softest hand touched his head.

Schmidt looked up. The nun's withered hand retreated. She gestured and turned to hold the door open to him. He rose, gathered his sword, and passed through the portal. Silent, the nun took him into the heart of the Klarissenkloster.

Inside was another nun sitting at a desk. This one younger than the first, yet still ancient. The silent nun gestured to a stool for Schmidt to sit. "Please forgive Mia. She made a vow of silence and has kept it for more decades than one can imagine. I am Rosina. What brings you here, Meister Schmidt?"

"I fear. I fear I have sold my soul to the Devil."

This declaration struck a laugh from the nun. She caught sight of Schmidt's grave face, "Forgive me, Frantz. It is said that all Henkers have sold their souls to the Devil."

"Yes," said Schmidt. "But, I fear my story is more than the common one."

"What would you have us do? We are but nuns," said Rosina.

"I do not know," said Schmidt. "I know only that no other house of worship or minion of God would open a door to me."

"Wait here," said Rosina. She gathered the skirts of her habit and disappeared through a narrow door behind her. A short time later she returned. "Follow me." Down a twisting corridor then out a portal into the apse of a church. Schmidt gazed nervously about. He'd never set foot inside a church. He felt unclean. The large sword in his hand seemed a blasphemy in such a place. She led him to a confessional. He entered and sat on the stool. Rosina slid shut the screen. After a wait, he heard a man's tread outside. Through the cane, he could not make out a face, but he did catch sight of aged hands and a plain wooden paternoster swinging free. He heard the other screen close.

"Rosina says you have a spiritual ailment."

Schmidt shook with emotion. "Where should I begin?"

"How about you start with" the gentle voice said, "'Forgive me for I have sinned.'"

Frantz made his confession.

It was full dark before Schmidt crossed the Hangman's Bridge again. Amman met him at the door. "I've sent the children to my wife. But we must deal with this." Ammon held forth a basket—the same basket in which Maria kept eggs. By candlelight Schmidt looked within. Inside, a tiny homunculus: half-formed with cloven hoofs and horned head. The face, the face of Potter Freddy. The monster was still-born not an hour before—the time of his confession. Amman stopped the bleeding and Maria was alive and sleeping.

They weighted the basket with stones. In the dark of Easter morning, they sunk the vessel with its unholy burden into the Pegnitz from the Hangman's Bridge.

Maria healed. Yet she held a sadness in her eyes. Schmidt could not console Maria's feeling that she was at fault for the loss. Schmidt knew the fault was his own.

A message arrived from Bamberg. Schmidt's father Heinrich has passed. The spring flowers were at full bloom when another letter arrived. Heinrich's widow had also passed away. The remaining estate to be shared among Frantz and his sister. That was spring.

Summer was worse. A pestilence of biting black flies descended upon Nuremberg. Then plague. No more executions until October. Thousands died. Amman struggled to remove the corpses. Schmidt and Amman ended up dumping most of the dead into the Pegnitz to float downstream. The waters were not fast, and the bodies piled up on the banks in heaps. The flies grew thicker. Margaretha caught the plague and died. Then Vitus. Only little Jorg survived. Without his journal, Schmidt could not recall the few floggings he performed over that awful summer: rapists, whores, thieves, lechers. The summer spent lancing buboes, and bleeding fevers away. None of it seemed to matter. There were still penances to pay despite the grace bestowed upon him on the eve of Easter.

Summers and winters tumbled forth like the waters of a river overflowing an ice dam. Or, alternatively, like a shattered mill wheel spinning haphazard in the waters. Work proceeded. The usual parade of whores and thieves flogged out of town. The occasional hanging. Fingers cut off. An ear cut off. Small mercies of beheading rather than strangling—one botched. Two executions by the wheel, both to thieves who had tortured woman with fire. Schmidt was numbed by it all. Maria silently went about her duties. The missing hub of Vitus and Margaretha threatened to throw Schmidt's and Maria's lives into separate arcs. Drown them in different streams. They were too intertwined, as the limbs of a corpse in the spokes of the wheel, to be separated. Jorg grew and, in growing, became flotsam upon which they clung.

Years wheeled by after Schmidt first made his winter trip to the hut on the river's edge.

When Maria gave birth to another daughter, they christened the girl Rosina. Due to his position, Schmidt could not attend the ceremony. He waited outside the church. Everything has but one end, only a sausage has two. Yet, there were also beginnings.

INGENUE

Alexander Palacio

So gracious were her hosts that the first bite, coming in that dreamy and timeless envelope before dawn, meant nothing to the girl. Her hostess, a graceful woman who wore her hair in a single plait, took and held to her lips the arm of the girl's date. He was a fat young man in a golf shirt of shimmery green fabric that clashed horribly with the embroidery of the loveseat. Her host, a tall gentleman with a pianist's elegant hands, glanced over from where he sat among the other guests and raised an eyebrow in amusement. The girl wondered if she should laugh, or object, or look away politely. She stared at her bare feet, wondering when she had lost her shoes. She waited to understand.

The girl had no real claim on the man, she supposed. He had introduced himself at a reception following a performance of *Die Zauberflöte*. He was effusive in his compliments and insistent that she join him for a dinner party at the home of certain friends of his who, he was sure, were great benefactors of the opera. "This is a couple well positioned to advance your career," he said. She had thought him charming, if perhaps a little smug. And perhaps her flash of possessiveness was premature, but the intimacy of the hostess's touch stung, nonetheless.

The hostess's teeth broke through skin and fat and muscle and fascia. The woman tore her mouth away from the girl's date. The hostess's hair remained undisturbed though her mouth was stained. The girl stared. Her date jerked his arm free and screamed. Another guest clambered drunkenly to his feet. Their host then came among them. He snapped another guest's arm below the elbow and tore out threads of meat from the exposed bone with his teeth. Blood splashed his merlot smoking jacket and darkened the suede of his opera slippers.

Men and women jostled and fought to enter the hall through which they had come, only to be dragged back into the salon screaming by the host or the hostess. Those that lived, those who stumbled out of the salon bearing the marks of teeth and claws, bore with them the knowledge of the sight of their hosts at their sport. The stampede of panicked flesh carried the girl into the hall, out of sight of her hosts By glimpses, the girl caught sight of her hosts in the midst of still bodies. They shivered with pleasure. They began to change. Bones clicked and lengthened, skin stretched and thickened, coarse hair sprouted, eyes bulged and gleamed red in the lamplight.

"Move!" screamed the fat man in the shimmery green golf shirt. He shouldered his way past the girl, clutching his bleeding arm as he pushed his way down the hall. She fell against the wainscoting, stumbled over a small console table, sent a vase of foxgloves to shatter against the silk runner carpet. The girl straightened and threw herself forward again. She wondered whether she should try to return to the foyer. The fat man trampled the other guests. The girl followed.

The hallway grew smaller and smaller as it went. It was not the corridor narrowing, she realized. The fat man was growing fatter. His frame shifted, growing even more bloated and distended and disproportionate. The fat man raised his bloodied arm to his face and stared in disbelief as it lengthened and inflated into something monstrous. His fingers merged and his nails broadened and his skin thickened; she heard sharp cracks and vicious grinding as an additional joint formed.

The other guests underwent distortion too, their limbs and torsos splitting and reforming, taking on carnival proportions. The girl stared at her own hand. It remained as it ever was. Her hand trembled. Then a clatter of hooves came from behind her and a pale mare galloped into the hall. In the long and haughty face and the plaited mane, the girl recognized the hostess. The mare's bloody teeth closed on the neck of a foppish elderly man. She thought she knew him from the opera, but it was impossible to say as his jaw split into insectoid mandibles, as his eyes doubled and quadrupled into the beady black eyes of a spider. The mare dragged the foppish man back into the salon screaming, his uncontrolled transformations continuing even as he grasped at the runner carpet.

Now, the guests ran. Some fell as their bodies changed. Others were taken by the hostess, or by the host, who coursed through the halls and rooms and alcoves in the shape of a great black stallion. Blood streaked the fleur-de-lis wallpaper. Where the stallion or the mare could not fit, the host and the hostess reverted to more humanoid shapes, naked and incomplete, but furnished with grasping claws and raking teeth.

After a time, the guests came to a large bay window facing the dark and empty street. The fat man, now having split his green golf shirt and only recognizable by the bite mark on the distal segment of his elongated and bulbous arm, forced his bulk against the window frame until the wood splintered and the glass cracked. He thrust his hands, which had now merged and swollen into something like the heavy pads of an elephant, through the glass. The shards lacerated his mutating limbs as he forced them through the opening and vanished into the foggy night.

Other guests, the few who had not been taken by the host and hostess, twisting into protean abominations, followed.

With the thunder of hooves they were present again, their strong jaws clamping shut, their muscled legs dragging the final few guests through halls filled with the detritus of once-charming décor, over a bergère chair now reduced to a mound of broken splinters and stained jacquard, into the salon where they had recently enjoyed elegant music and charades. A cheery fire still burned. One guest's thrashing arms elongated, uncoiling like a jack-in-the-box spring to fill the narrow hallway as the hostess dragged him away. His flailing hand struck the sconce, shattering the bulbs, darkening the hall and foyer where the girl pressed into an unobtrusive corner. She checked the pale skin of her arms, felt the flesh of her neck and face. It was unmarred, unbroken. She was glad for the midnight blue of her dress. The house was silent. How long, she wondered, could she remain in this shadowed corner of the foyer? She stared at the broken window, the tantalizing empty street beyond, the iron-clouded sky above. From the hall she thought she heard a snort, the scrape of a hoof.

Then another sound—a prickly tapping, a leathery creak. The girl looked up to see the hostess creeping along the ceiling, her pale human limbs splitting and doubling and darkening, her torso segmenting into the bulbous arachnoid thorax, shrinking quickly as she descended from a strand of silk to wait between the mouth of the hallway and the door. The little spider vanished in the darkness; a strand of silk shone silver when it caught the moonlight.

The girl waited longer, unmoving, watching the spider from the shadows. The scent of rain was real. As was the touch of clean air on her shoulders. Only the broken window and the spider floating in the foyer kept the horror in her memory.

The fog began to lift and the sky outside to lighten. The heavens' blues and oranges tinged the bellies of the long clouds that crossed the horizon from the east. The girl took her chance. She sprinted across the foyer. She dove through the broken window in a single liquid motion. The cobbles, worn flat with age, were cold and hard and wet with dew on her bare feet. Again, she wished she had her shoes.

Dawn bathed her bare shoulders, her sweat-lankened hair, her wrinkled and dusty dress. The house's front door opened from the inside. The hostess stood at the threshold, smiling. Her face was clean, her clothing neat, her plaited hair immaculate.

"Thank you for coming," the hostess said. "I'm sorry we didn't have more time to chat. I hope you enjoyed your evening. Your date certainly seemed to. Perhaps when he recovers from his distemper he'll bring you back for another visit. My husband and I would enjoy the chance to become better acquainted."

The girl glanced down at her feet. A small black spider scuttled toward her. She crushed the spider with her heel, bruising it against the hard cobbles. She looked back up at her hostess in the doorway, her shoulders square, a fierce light in her eyes.

"I think I have just acquainted myself with your husband," the girl said. "Please be sure I will acquaint myself with you when we meet again."

The hostess's face tightened to a porcelain mask. Slowly, a brittle smile cracked across her lips.

"Hospitality is dead," the hostess whispered.

INQUISITION OF DER SCHLEIM

JB Jackson

Rough translation from the German by Randall Kelso of an anonymous, undated (after 1628) manuscript. Basham & Winstead (San Francisco). De re dordica: Items from the Seaberg Society. December 8, 1997. Sale no. 818, Lot 55. Provenance: Calvin "Cal" Calhoun.

The scoundrel had been found among the smoldering embers of the town house of Meister Durchdenmeer, alias 'The Foreigner.' At the time of his seizure, he would only say he was called Der Schleim, lately of Stab. Nor would he confess what he was doing there. I paid off the watchman, the so-called landlord of the Green Frog, that I may go see Der Schleim down in in his cell. The sum was high but fair.

"My report is to be laid before the Rat tomorrow morn so pray do not hinder me!" I said. But the watchman was too busy counting by the light of an oil lamp the stacks of gleaming florins heaped upon his table.

A steep staircase of worn stone led downward to a maze of damp dungeon passageways. I made my way in the gloom, treading into the echoes of my own footsteps. I stopped when I came to a cell door upon which was a crowing cock painted fiery red. The mark of an incendiary. Der Schleim's presence oozed through the door. Apart from my taper, the only light came from a smoky brazier of burning coals in a nearby alcove. I took a seat upon a small stool of oak brought for the occasion. I drew my cowl close about my face then opened the rusty iron grate. With my gloved hand I placed within the dark opening an apple.

Chains clanked across the floor. A subtle mouldering reek filled my nostrils. The apple was removed. The fruit was replaced by the pox-ravaged face of Der Schleim. His round, inquisitive eyes regarded my cloaked figure with great curiosity. The prisoner would be heavily ironed at the waist and feet. Behind him would be an oaken bunk and perhaps a rough blanket. Next to that, a bench and large wooden sanitary bucket fitted with a lid that served as a table. Naught else. As I well knew.

Der Schleim stroked the apple before biting into it gingerly, as if it hurt his teeth. "You are the *Lochschöffen*, come to hear my statement?" he said eagerly. He moved the bench over to the door and sat down with a grunt. Der Schleim's cheerful tone was at odds with the dismal surroundings.

My answer was, after removing my gloves, to withdraw a portable lap desk from my bag and unfold it. This contraption interested the prisoner greatly. His eyes followed my hands as I seated my taper, then prepared my parchment, quill, and ink. Assuming I was the *Lochschöffen* and the examination a mere formality, I found the prisoner to be forthcoming. One will do anything to break the abiding dreariness of solitary confinement.

"They are sending me to Turm," uttered Der Schleim, merrily. "They granted me a respite on account of a lack of proof."

"Tell me about your hump," I said, readying my quill. If they were indeed sending the wretch to Turm, it was because of his frailty.

"Born a mooncalf, I was," he said, speaking with his mouth full. He snorted loudly but it was not enough to stanch the snot cascading down his beard. "My mother took one look at me and wrung my neck. A hook-maker hooked me out of the manure pit. He and his wife took me in and raised me. Most cruel, they were. Especially the hook-maker. I stayed because of my feet.

"One fine day, the hook-maker was found upon one of his own hooks. No one thought to blame me but the hook-maker's wife was questioned. Afterward, she vowed never to set eyes upon me again and sent me on my way. Kicked around, I was, a ward of the town. Friendless, penniless, and witless. Because a boy has to eat, I became a thief. The good town folk showed me no mercy. If my hump and feet were not awful enough, they clipped my ears and took a finger from each hand. Der Schleim, they called me."

"And what of your nose?" I said.

"Born thus, was I."

"What of your previous careers?"

"Hook-maker," said Der Schleim. He paused, as if trying to remember if he had ever earned his keep by honest means. "Hook-maker," he repeated, decidedly.

"Tell me about your partnership with Durchdenmeer and the happenstance of your meeting," I said.

"I was caught unlawfully partaking of the *Bauermeister*'s beehives. Fancy that, would you. A man who thinks he owns the honeybees!" Der Schleim sniffed derisively.

"After I was flogged out of the village, I went back and burned it down. While I watched the rising flames and listened to the anguished screams of my tormentors, I rooted through their homes. My pockets jingled with gold. My bags were bursting with booty. I slew the *Armendiener*'s daughter. Then, with my cudgel of birchwood, I dealt with her lustily."

Der Schleim paused and looked at me searchingly, as if waiting for a gasp. I adjusted my cowl. "Obrist Holky would have been so proud," he continued. Der Schleim turned his head and blasted phlegm out of two slits where his nose should be. The rough stone masonry of the cell was crusty with his green and brown snot.

"Lost, I was. I wandered until I found a little

oakwood near Thennalohe. I made my home there. I learned to fend for myself. With my bare hands I became skilled at fishing and hunting. Cows, spiders, toads. However, the easiest prey were other hunters.

"When I was seen sacking a fresh corpse, I fled the little oakwood I called home. What was to become of me, I knew not. In Lambretzhoffen, I bashed an official on the head with a stone cannonball and took his signet ring. The landlord has it now. I broke the back of another as he drank from the fountain at Feylsdorf. His cloak and forty-four florins I kept for myself. From a carrier I stole nine ducats and a cheese, leaving him face down in the Floß."

"And of Durchdenmeer?" I said, impatiently.

"Near the Schleegasse at Hersspruch I lay in wait under a bridge. By the dim light of the gloaming I beheld a wayfarer in a pointy hat. As the shadowy figure crossed the bridge, I came out from my hiding place, meaning to strike from behind. No sooner had I raised my cudgel, my prey turned and grasped my arm. With dreadful strength he lifted me by my neck and held me aloft. Over three ells in height, he was.

In the dim light I regarded Der Schleim's grimy stump of a neck and wondered how anyone could get a firm grip on it.

"I grasped at my prey's pointy hat and clawed at his beard. Having already taken what I swore was my last breath, I kicked with my clubbed feet until I fainted. Yet I lived. When

I came to, I was sprawled next to a campfire on which bubbled a cauldron. The wayfarer peered at me through a haze of smoke rings. His pipe was fashioned out of a long piece of bone. He gestured to the cauldron with it. I joined him in a hearty meal of *Schnitz* with mutton of the likes I had never tasted.

"After supping my fill, I gave thanks and introduced myself. He uttered only the name 'Durchdenmeer,' which I took to be a seafarer's name. When he saw that I had only three fingers on each hand, he laughed like a kobold. I did not understand and laughed, too, like a kobold.

"After such a meal, I slept through the night as a newborn. I opened my eyes to the sweet melody of 'Es wollt ein Jäger jagen.' When I sat up in wonder the man stopped blowing his gemshorn and gave me bread. He then gathered his belongings and rose to leave. He beckoned me to follow and I obeyed. We stayed for a spell at Stab. At the Inn of the Reichsapfel. Then to Nürnberg we went. There we dwelled and I became his procurer."

"A procurer of women?" I said.

"Durchdenmeer seldom spoke. Rather, he gave me lists of things to bring to him. At first, these things were easy to gain. Herbs and spices, and the like. These I supposed were for cooking though we usually took our meals together at the Tatzelwurm or sometimes the Ass. Some were stinky. Devil's dung I should not like to smell again. Nor *Hundskamille*. And some, such as savin and hemlock, are deadly poisons.

"He gave me money for these things, and often a little more for my trouble. When I could, I pilfered what he wanted then pocketed the coins. In the beginning we stayed at the Drei Kronen but soon moved into a cozy town house in the Barfüßer quarter. Durchdenmeer I never knew to sleep. Indeed at night, I often heard low murmuring, or bells tinkling from his chambers. Sometimes I beheld spectral lights of many colors dancing from beneath his door. Once, when his door was ajar, a rush of air extinguished my taper and I heard voices other than the Meister's from within. At no time was I allowed to enter."

"Did you or Durchdenmeer ever hurt anyone?" I said.

"One time," said Der Schleim, "the Meister bade me bring him a spleen. I knew in my heart he wanted a human spleen, but I asked not wherefore or whence I should find one. From the Elendegasse, I prowled the Lorenzer side of town in the morning and the Sebalder side all night, wringing my hands. On the second day I ventured without the city walls as far as the old Rabenstein, not knowing what I should do. But on the second night I reaped the spleen of an infant found along the Fischbach. This, I laid at the Meister's feet. He seemed much vexed. He accepted it nonetheless and for my trouble gave me a three-fingered punch ring that fit my hand well.

"Later I was given charms with which to lure young women, for I am too ugly to do so of my own. The Meister taught me well how to wield them.

"The first luckless Fräulein, a whore with flaxen hair called Hedwig, I found outside the pig market where whores like to linger. She raised such a ruckus all the way back to the house. After the Meister bade her come into his chambers the noise was ended.

"Whensoever I should please the Meister with a thing hard to come by, he sometimes gave me a bounty. After I brought him Hedwig, that night he gave me new feet. Another time, a magical coin which always came back to me. Until the landlord took that too, curse him."

"New feet?" I said, quizzically.

With almost comical effort, Der Schleim turned in his chair and held up both of his filthy feet for me to see. As were his hands, Der Schleim's feet were heavily ironed, but I could see nothing wrong with them. They were, in fact, the least afflicted aspects of his body. Nicely formed and oddly small and youthful for such an otherwise sickly person.

"To Hedwig I have always believed they belonged," Der Schleim said with no emotion. He looked down and sighed deeply before continuing. "Still, I brought to the Meister the young women. As many as seventeen or eighteen over half as many moons. Many of these came from the riding school on Schütt Island. The Meister scolded me for stalking so close to home. Heeding his warning, I sought others as far as the Johannisfriedhof or the Frauen-Thor. As with Hedwig, they were brought to the Meister's house where they passed from all memory. But for one. A peasant wench who called herself Ursula."

The name excited me. I stopped writing and leaned in closer, almost gagging from the stench.

"One night the Meister sent me to the old convent library behind the church of St. Katharina. The library was forgotten, he said, and the books would not be missed. Behind this place was a peaceful apple orchard. After I had nicked the books, I lingered in this grove with a jug and a pipe.

"Under the light of the full moon, I caught sight of something that made me blink and rub my eyes with wonder. In a clearing lay a Fräulein, naked as the day she was born except for her stockings. She rested upon her elbows, legs spread wide as if beckoning to her beloved. '*Eine Hexe*,' I said to myself, though I had never seen one before."

At this remark, I smiled sardonically.

Der Schleim licked his lips. "Beguiled I was by her long, dark hair, which as a waterfall fell upon her shoulders and tits. Her milk-white skin shone under the moonlight like a snowy, rolling meadow. I would have lain with her then and there, had not a thick fog moved in. Like Venus come from the sea, the witch rose to her feet, yawned, and stretched as a person waking up of a morning well rested. She brushed dirt off her backside and the leaves from her tresses while I ogled her breathlessly. She pulled a smock over her head then deftly leaped over the wall. Alone was I, breeches undone, pipe in hand.

"On the hangman's bridge I caught up to the witch and brought out the charms. She took my wrist and said, 'Put those away.' I bade her come with me back to the house. So taken with her was the Meister, he kept her to cook and clean. She was given my room. In a vaulted undercroft where goods were stored I now lay my head. This sudden twist of fate unsettled me. The first night, she lay still and quiet when in the buttery I cornered her and availed myself of her body."

At this I bristled but held my tongue.

"The witch had a way of getting whatsoever she wanted. She would brazenly catch the cloak of the Meister when he came through the door of an evening. It was not long before she was allowed into the Meister's chambers. I dropped to my knees and begged her, 'Tell me what you have seen!'

"'Never!' she cackled. When I pinched her under her smock she lunged for a spindle then stabbed it into my ear hole. Into my other ear hole she hissed 'You are a gruesome, thieving, snaggle-toothed *Wechselbalg*. You sicken me.' She said that should I ever so much as dream of her tasty sex again she would cut out my tongue and add it to the *Schnitz*. After I struggled to my feet, I spat at her and cried, 'Away, black-brows!'

"From that day forward, I satisfied my lust elsewhere, employing the charms the Meister gave me. My wrath I would save for the witch.

"Of the Meister I saw less and less," continued Der Schleim. "When I did, his mien was such that I dare not look at him lest he turn me into a toad. This he threatened whenever he thought I had swindled him." He paused to consider this last statement before chuckling, "Oh, he had no inkling!"

"What became of the women?" I said. I knew well what happened but wanted to hear what Der Schleim would say. He merely shrugged.

"Tell me more about Ursula, then," I said. "Did you love her?"

Der Schleim considered this question carefully. "I did not like to," he replied, at last. "When the witch wanted something, she plied me with white wine sweetened with flowers and herbs and was playful. Many times I found myself scrubbing the chamber pots, my loins aflame without understanding." Der Schleim rubbed his hands together thoughtfully, then crossed his legs.

"My itch for the witch would not be scratched. Of the keyhole to her chamber I made good use. So careful was I not to give myself away on the creaky threshold, I dared not breathe. At bedtime the witch would undress and face the mirror. From the bottles on her vanity she would apply the scented oils. To her neck, breasts, armpits, and navel. And to her sex. Next to which I descried the mark of the devil. Thus I spilled my seed on her doorstep many an evening.

"When the witch went to the market, I often slipped into her chamber. Apart from bottles of aloe, labdanum, and storax found upon her vanity, there was naught of worth save a carved boxwood comb which I broke when I tried to run it through my matted rat's nest. I was scared, so I tossed the comb out the window.

"After searching high and low, I at last pulled from under a floorboard a silken bundle which held manifold items: candles and incense, a small knife, a goblet, a talisman upon a chain, and other things besides. These she must have employed in her dark arts. There were also a number of small books filled with strange signs."

"Did Durchdenmeer have any idea with whom he was dealing?" I said.

"That he had a witch on his hands? If so, he did not say." Der Schleim paused to take another bite of apple.

"Whensoever the moon was full," he continued, while chewing noisily, "she would sneak from the house to the old convent grove and lie, as before, naked on her back but for her stockings. And the talisman about her neck, which she sometimes clutched. Always I followed and lusted after her from the shadows.

"The day of a full moon, the Meister was called away to München. The witch begged him to take her but was denied. How I laughed in her face! I was to go with him as his servant, but then he denied me as well. Now it was the witch who laughed.

"As soon as the Meister had closed the door behind him, the witch accused me of nicking her comb. She brought a kettle down on my head. Already as a newborn I had escaped the Dunkle Großmutter's clutches. I was not about to let this one take me without a fight. Limb from limb I would have torn her, but all of a sudden I had a clever thought.

"After the witch went to lie un-Christianlike under the moon, I sought the old Meistersinger who lived nearby. A more God-fearing man there never was. From his dormer above the orchard he laid eyes on the witch's snatch and bawled, 'What is the meaning of this?'

"'You see what I see,' was my reply, wherefore the Meistersinger sounded the alarm.

"As the Meistersinger's henchmen laid hands on her, the witch turned to me and shrieked, 'May your worthless God guard you! For dealing with me thus you will see me again one day.'

"No sooner was the witch dragged away, biting and hissing, I sought her smock. To my nostrils I held the garment, which was still warm, and took in all her odors."

Der Schleim stopped speaking and turned his head away from me. He took another bite of apple, which he chewed pensively.

"As I made to leave," he continued, "I beheld in the dirt a gleam. It was the talisman from the witch's neck. This, I hid carefully under a cobblestone near the sundial, upon which I marked an *S* with my magic coin."

"An *S*?" I said, scribbling quickly.

"*Für den Schleim,*" he wheezed. Here I noticed that one corner of Der Schleim's mouth is higher than the other in a sort of a fixed sneer.

"Back at the house, I lost no time picking the lock to the Meister's chambers. Now was my chance to take a good look. To pry and poke around to my heart's delight. I may not have a nose, but that does not mean I am not nosy." Der Schleim grinned hideously at his own joke. His laugh turned into a harsh cough.

"What did you find within Durchdenmeer's chambers?" I persisted.

"A bewildering array of instruments adorned a large table comprising a thick quartz slab upon an oaken base. I will not say I knew what they all were, but one I understood to be a distilling apparatus. Next to it stood an hourglass whose sands were in motion. Within a large jar of toads I fancied I saw myself. Shelves sagged under the weight of books and scrolls, many of them ancient and worm eaten. Whence the Meister came by these things I wondered greatly for we came to Nürnberg empty-handed.

"Beyond this workshop, there was a smaller, windowless room well-stocked with bottles and vials bearing kelp, scullcap, or bark of the pussy willow. The label of one read 'Tooth of a Khul.' It was empty. Some of the bottles bore labels written in an unknown tongue. Others bore no labels at all. In the corner stood a hogshead of riesling. I fetched an empty flask then lowered it into the barrel. Thus, I slaked my thirst well and then some.

"An urn held my old feet. Nearby, a cloth

which, when removed, betrayed a large jar containing the head of Hedwig, mouth agape. Her flaxen curls waved spectrally like river grass in an oily, opaline fluid. Of this I will say no more.

"A prism I pinched, thinking the Meister would not miss it. Sorely tempted was I by a ball of crystal within which swirling clouds beckoned. A curtain of green velvet concealed a small door covered in studded leather through which the Meister would have had to stoop. This lock took much longer to pick. It was not until the deepest part of the night that I gained ingress into a small, pentagonal chamber, also windowless. To my dismay, it was empty but for a chair with straps within a circle drawn upon the floor in salt.

"With my ransacking I carried on, determined to make the most of my good luck. At last I found what I had only hoped for: two glimmering ingots of purest gold."

Here, Der Schleim closed his eyes as if relishing the memory of this joyful moment.

"These I caressed then held to my cheeks. So cool to the touch were they! Their heft I weighed in my hands. I cracked them together and clicked my heels with glee. A jig I danced! How my heart leaped at the thought of beating the Meister at his own game. To Augsburg I would go! Where they know well what to do with gold."

Der Schleim lowered his head and appeared to be quietly sobbing.

"Too much I drank," he said, almost inaudibly. "The Meister found me curled in the corner of his workshop, swathed in the green velvet curtain. He lifted from me the prism and the gold ingots. When he asked where Ursula was I blurted that she had been carried away. At this news, the Meister's face turned white, then red. He besought me to tell all lest he turn me into a toad. But I was afraid! He yanked me into the back room and strapped me to the chair within the circle of salt.

"He left me for hours in that dark room. I could hear the Meister pacing, mumbling, and cursing. At last, he shouted 'Der Schleim!'" This was followed by a loud crash. He burst through the door with red-hot tongs. When he brandished them in my face I wailed."

Der Schleim began to retch pitifully. He waved me off when I leaned forward to get a closer look. Presently, he composed himself and now glanced at me sideways. Foam had collected on his lips. He wiped his mouth with his sleeve.

Der Schleim continued. "With the red-hot tongs the Meister nipped me on the elbows and knees. 'Hark! How the devil whines,' he cried, until I told all as I am telling you now.

"When there was nothing left to tell, the Meister gagged me with a stocking and again forsook me. With my tongue I wiggled the socking until it fell onto my lap. I yelled until I was without speech. The leathern straps I pulled at until my wrists and ankles were raw meat. Until there were sores on my buttocks I squirmed. My lips peeled from thirst and my stomach fed upon itself. I soiled myself and stewed in it. Whether it was day or night I knew not, nor how many days had passed.

"Something came snuffling around my lovely new toes. A glimmer of hope, I had, when I was able to wrest one hand free. When the snuffler began to crawl up my leg, I waited calmly. When it was within reach, I seized it and devoured it. But I hungered still. Just when I could stand to live no longer, the old Meistersinger came with his henchmen.

"I was unstrapped and led roughly out into the workshop. 'Behold,' I said, feebly. 'A sorcerer dwells here! Meister Durchdenmeer has plundered these books from the old convent library.'

"'Liar!' called a voice from the doorway. It was the witch.

"'Lift your skirts!' I barked. 'Show them the mark of the Devil!'

"'I have come for what is mine,' she said. 'Where is it?'

"With a flourish I removed the cloth from the jar. 'Perhaps you come for the head of Hedwig, whore of the pig market!' I said, haughtily. The Meistersinger gasped, then pointed his bony finger at me."

Der Schleim was now drooling abundantly, having eaten the apple's core, seeds and all.

"The Meistersinger's men set upon me and beat me senseless," he slurred. "This nasty turn of events sapped my will to fight. When I regained my wits, the workshop had been ransacked and set afire. With my backside burning

I made my way into the hogshead of riesling and pulled the lid shut. The wine stung my wounds. There were times I thought my lungs might burst or that I would be boiled alive. Knowing these were my last moments on this earth, I buggered myself, then drank myself to sleep. Thus I was found before being hauled howling to this godforsaken place."

Der Schleim winced as if in pain, then vomited. With a trembling hand, he gripped the frame of the opening for support. His breathing was now labored.

"I was to be led away on the tumbril. Beheaded with a sword as a special favor on St. Walburga's Day..." Der Schleim gulped audibly before continuing. "An incendiary, they called me. But it was the witch, I tell you!"

Now, I lowered my cowl to reveal my face.

"You!" croaked Der Schleim. As his bloodshot eyes bulged accusingly from their sockets, the prisoner stiffened and his rotten teeth bared in an involuntary rictus. I watched vengefully as his convulsing body now sank limply against the door.

Reaching my gloved hand through the opening, with a forceps I gingerly recovered the apple stem from Der Schleim's slackened mouth. This I wrapped in a handkerchief and placed in my bag.

I gathered my belongings and calmly made my way through the maze of damp dungeon passageways. As I emerged from the staircase, I murmured to the watchman: "*Male patratis sunt atra theatra parata.*"

"And a very good evening to you, Fräulein," he laughed, greedily. The landlord of the Green Frog did not look up. He was still busy counting by the light of an oil lamp the stacks of gleaming florins heaped upon his table.

THE HANGING by Giovanni Domenico Tiepolo, 1790-1799, pen and brown ink, brush and brown washes over black chalk, 35.5 x 47.5 cm. Iris and B. Gerald Cantor Center for Visual Arts at Stanford University

WHAT KIND OF ARTIST IS JACK VANCE?

Paul Rhoads

My life has been exactly the opposite of what happens in novels where the heroine, born a simple peasant, ends up an illustrious princess. In my youth I was treated as a person of distinction; later I discovered that I was nothing, and had nothing.

—*Marguerite de Staal de Launay*

Iwant to loosen the stubborn link between Jack Vance and genre labels, rather than burden him with yet another. The danger cannot be avoided since we must communicate with words.

The painter Giandomenico Tiepolo (1727-1804) was the son of the more famous Gianbatista. Much of the son's career was spent as an assistant to his father, who was the author of one of those vast eighteenth-century oeuvres requiring an atelier. The late polymath, Harry Mathews, in defending the opinion that the younger Giandomenico's art is an inferior version of his father's, tries to define its particular character. The case is tough. Giandomenico's work owes so much stylistically to the elder Gianbatista that the untrained eye cannot tell them apart. Even connoisseurs have made errors that were only corrected by fortuitously-discovered documentation. Mathews points out that Giandomenico's work is neither a prolongation of the baroque style of his father—and the other Rubenists, then going out of fashion—nor an example of the resurgent classical style, of which Poussin was the hero. Searching for a word, Mathews chooses "naturalism."

The sense in which Mathews employs the term reminded me of Vance. (Note, naturalism should not be confused with realism—neither in the nineteenth century literary sense as applied to authors like Zola, nor in its designation of contemporary non-abstract painting— usually prefixed with "photo-," "hyper-,"or "optical-"). Literary realism, as Jules Lemaitre explains in *Les Contemporains*, is not more real than any other style, but rather its taste for the sordid. Realism's practitioners revel in a vision of man as brute, slave to unexamined and ignoble passions, oppressor or oppressed, all are part of a mechanistic world inspiring disgust. The style is an approach, a taste, not a privileged view with a claim on objective truth. For Lematire, it gives no better picture of life than another—it is even likely to carry an artist farther from reality than another style.

What then of Giandomenico's naturalism and how it applies to Jack Vance? Although, Mathews insists on writing about sex at the flimsiest opportunity, but of his thesis I retain this: Giandomenico's vision partakes of none of the special exaltations characteristic of either the baroque or classicism. It lacks both the divine excitement of his father's work and the noble repose of classicist, Poussin. Giandomenico *fils*'s personal works are usually classified as genre painting, meaning paintings of everyday life—a manner in which neither his father nor Poussin ever worked. Some of his paintings are indeed scenes of people at a fair, enjoying a picnic, a dance, an acrobatic display. Yet these paintings retain nothing of realism and its attendant disgust about them. They are tranquil and inviting. They are certainly not painted with any realist attention to detail. They are broadly and decoratively conceived, and—like his father's vast frescos of celestial beings cavorting in the clouds—executed with brio.

But many of Giandomenico's personal works should not be classified as genre scenes. Notably his ink and wash drawings called *Amusements for Children* (see p. 88 "A Hanging"). They show a world of Punchinellos, each with false humpback, big-nosed mask, and tall truncated-cone hat: in scene after scene, Punchinellos, male and female, young and old, engaged in every imaginable activity.

As Mathews points out, Giandomenico's treatment of these varied scenes offers no overt commentary.

There is one additional consideration before we proceed to Vance. Probably the most famous painting by Francisco Goya is *The Third of May, 1808* (see p. 104) depicting Napoleonic soldiers executing citizens of Madrid. One description I have read of this painting includes the phrase: "The execution squad consists of machine-like beings mercilessly slaughtering these martyrs for liberty." This image is regularly trotted out in the wearisome propaganda assault upon the horrors of war. Unlike Goya, Giandomenico does not give us an instructive spectacle of the forces of darkness expunging the children of light. Instead he presents, for example, an execution—one spectacle in the infinitely varied human comedy—Punchinello executes Punchinello. It has no more political weight than the game of *pétanque* among the Punchinellos. No matter how active Giandomenico's scenes, they are characterized by a certain serenity. Giandomenico's sublime vision, by a sort of divine indulgence, penetrates the hearts of men, contemplates their frail humanity, and looks beyond their sins to the sheer spectacle of the human drama.

Giandomenico's *Amusements for Children* reminds me of Vance's work. There is the same scope, serenity and absence of this-worldly passions. This does not mean that, any less than Giandomenico, Vance lacks opinions or positions but that they are tempered and nourished by a special outlook. But these are out-stripped by a particular sort of artistic nature which, though by no means equivalent, has something in common with philosophy. This is rare in the twentieth century. Only the likes of an Orwell or a Solzhenitsyn dare approach our idols without reverence, to poke at them, not aggressively but with the sympathetic ob-jectivity of a doctor. Vance is never polemical. He does not rush out to noisily confront the establishment—though, unintentionally, and sadly for his reputation, he constantly manag-es to step on incorrect toes.

Unlike Goya's *Third of May*, Vance does not present the world as a battleground of the chil-dren of darkness against the children of light. With Giandomenico and Vance we are, instead, given a variety of human beings who, howev-er contrasting their acts, are not fundamental-ly different of nature; at the deepest level, the worst among us are no less human than the best. Vance makes no secret of his opinions. If he takes sides, he takes is the side of Art. He is not above the fray—in the sense that he owns a superior insight which renders lesser insights meaningless. He is in it, as all honest folk are. But, whatever his personal convictions, his view of the world, tempered by an uncompro-mising willingness to see what humanity there is in anyone, is relieved not of political position but of political *passion*. Like Giandomenico, his outlook is broad and tranquil.

Take an only moderately hot topic: the death penalty. Vance, clearly, is not going to rush out and protest monstrous behavior meeting the ultimate penalty at the hands of legitimate forces of social order. This traditional attitude is fairly widespread and, as such, ought to be allowed a degree of respectability. Some, of course, regard capital punishment as unacceptable, and this opinion may likewise be admitted as respectable by those who disagree. But for some—and hotter issues illustrate this more neatly—the opposing side is not respectable, sometimes not even tolerable. The world, divided into children of light and darkness, fills with passion, contempt, rancor, then hate, and eventually civic violence.

How does Vance, the artist, treat this issue? From the macabre burlesque of *Clarges*, to the pathetic illusions of Dame Hester in *Ports of Call*, his œuvre proclaims the infinite preciousness of each fleeting moment of life. In fact, if Vance's message had to be summed up in a single phrase, it would probably be "Savor the present," or some other injunction to the same effect. Certainly something warmer and more urgent, than *carpe diem*. In Vance, death is rarely the mere plot point of murder mysteries, the mere decor of westerns. It is never gratuitous, always poignant. Throughout his work the sense of mortality, if not actually present, is never distant and often rises to a crescendo. Take this passage from The Killing Machine, its striking phrase pronounced by the person in all Vance's œuvre most preoccupied with mortality: the hormagaunt Kokor Hekkus—here disguised as Seuman Otwal:

Otwal laughed negligently.
"You just saved his life."
"I saved our second payment,"
said Gersen, "because I would have
been forced to kill you as well."
"No matter, no matter. Let us not talk
of death, horrid to consider nonbeing!"

In *The Green Pearl* Vance takes pains to acquaint us with Sir Hune and make him sympathetic. Then Sir Hune violates the new law.
In a scene graven in the memories of all Vance
readers Aillas marches to Three Pines house
and invests the places:

Sir Hune had pulled up his gate
and waited glumly for the summons
to parley. He waited in vain, while
with sinister efficiency the Troice
contingents made their preparations.
(Three Pines is bombarded).
Sir Hune was dumbfounded and
outraged; where was the call to parley he
had so confidently expected? And he liked
even less the sight of the gibbet which
was being erected somewhat to the side.
It was strong and high, and well braced,
as if prepared for much heavy work.

Sir Hune and his collaborators are forced
out of their fort with fire and cut down with
arrows:

Some of the warriors leaped erect and fought with swords until they too were shot dead by the Troice archers; others were captured as they lay stunned in the bracken, and among these was Sir Hune. His arms were bound; a rope was tied around his neck and he was dragged stumbling to the gibbet. Aillas stood at a distance of twenty yards. For the briefest of moments the two looked eye to eye, then Sir Hune was hoisted high.

This act of swift, brutal justice is recounted with typical Vancian economy. Only the moment of eye contact recalls us to Sir Hune's full humanity. It is sufficient! But Vance is not done; Sir Hune's guilt turns out to be deeper than we realized, a revelation which comes later. Meanwhile, Aillas conducts the following drama:

The remaining prisoners, some fifty men, stood haggard and woebegone, waiting their turn. Aillas went to inspect them. He spoke: "In point of law you, like your leaders, are rebels. Probably you deserve hanging. However, I deplore the waste of strong men, who should be supporting the cause of their country rather than working to defeat it. I offer each of you an option. You may be hanged at this moment, or you may enlist in the king's army, to serve him with full loyalty.

Choose! Those who wish to be hanged,
let them step yonder to the gibbet."
There were uneasy mutters, a shifting
of feet, and wall-eyed glances toward
the gibbet, but no one moved.

No great surprise! They want to live! The
reader is feeling the full force of that desire.
We are here given a second look at death, this
time through the eyes of those who have just
escaped it. Now, a new situation arises:

Sir Tristano returned with grisly news.
"[…] No one survives in the house, save
only those in the dungeons. I counted
eight prisoners and three torturers;
then I could no longer bear the stench."
Aillas' heart went cold. "Torturers then?
I might have suspected as much […]"

The Vancian touch, revealing the whole of
Aillas' interior, to say nothing of what we learn
of Sir Hune. The malefactors and victims are
brought forth:

The three torturers stood apart, surly,
uncertain, but feigning a disdainful
detachment from the situation […] The
third, who seemed no more than Aillas'
own age, smiled with unconvincing
bravado first out at the troops, then
up at the bodies on the gibbet […]
"Sergeant! Hoist high these three horrors."

"Hold!" cried the young torturer
Luton in a sudden sweat. "We obeyed
orders, no more! Had we not done
so, a dozen others would have leapt
forward to take over our posts!"
"And today they would dangle
from the gibbet instead of you [...]
Sergeant, take them aloft."
"Hurrah!" quavered Nols…

Vance's telling, always brief and to the point, makes the blood run cold. Opponents of the death penalty are brought face to face with both the high reasoning and low impulses which weigh on the fate of the likes of Sir Hune and Luton. Poor Nols, tortured for months by men who have neglected their own humanity, cheers the execution. Who can blame him? On the other hand, in the midst of all this, and with the lightest indications, Vance invades us with the dreadful sensation which traverses the foolish Luton; we will not escape the scene without empathy. Luton's death comes as a jolt. Only Nols and his fellows, perhaps made of no better stuff than Luton, gasp out a cheer. Aillas and the Troice are mute.

How does Vance do it? What do we know of Luton? First, his name. Then, he is Aillas's own age. Why not just say he is young? Vance equates them: Luton, like Aillas, is the center and hero of the story of his own unfolding life—most of which, normally, lies before him. In Luton's bravado we see his anxiety. He is fascinated by the mortal menace around him. Then the sudden sweat, the desperate argument—a series of deft strokes—and the death of Luton becomes unforgettable, a humanizing reminder of the personhood of every individual, however puny or despicable. Though Luton is as evil as you like, evil in an easy and horrific manner, he is yet a person. How much deeper a message than Goya's scene, where the soldiers are soulless instruments of oppression, humanity a status reserved only for victims. Giandomenico and Vance see humanity everywhere, in the killers and the killed, the good and the evil.

This is no relativism, no moral neutrality; good and evil are not given short shrift. The unjust are justly sanctioned by the just. And the unjust persecute the just unjustly. Justice, though given her due, gives way to larger issues, the equalizing passion for life. Vance will not allow us to traverse these scenes without a torn heart. The spirit that animates the episode at Three Pines House is the same that animates Giandomenico's hanging. We are shown an event. A sad, even tragic event, but a human kind of event which must ultimately be seen in the context of the warp and woof of human experience. This does not exalt it but does drain it of aspects of the passion it might excite, so that it can point beyond them to larger truths and questions.

So much for controversial subjects. What of the opposite, something banal, like romance? Again, we encounter Vance's naturalism. Perhaps the most characteristic Vancian romance is that of Aillas and Tatzel, which occurs in two episodes. First, Aillas is enslaved at Castle Sank, where he becomes entranced with princess Tatzel. To her Aillas is invisible, a sub-human cipher. Later, he captures her. Together they trek across Dahaut to North Ulfland, where Aillas restores her to her father's protection. How can this romance be classified? It is certainly not romantic! Nor does it have a well-rounded beginning, middle, and end. Nor is the story tragic, like *Romeo and Juliet*, nor comic, like *Emma*. Nor is it realist, as nothing sordid happens; in fact, hardly anything happens at all—which excludes the energetic and busy baroque. The outcome is simply what would naturally happen, an opportunity for further characterization:

> Thinking back to his time at Castle Sank, Aillas tried to remember his first sight of Tatzel: then a slender creature of thoughtless assurance walking with long swaggering strides by reason of natural verve.
>
> Aillas sighed. Upon a heartsick young man, Tatzel, with her fascinating face and jaunty vitality, had made a deep impression.
>
> And now? He watched her as she worked. Her assurance had been replaced by sullen unhappiness, and the bitter facts of her present existence had taken the luster from her verve.

Tatzel felt the pressure of his attention and turned a quick glance over her shoulder. "Why do you look at me so?"

"An idle whim."

Tatzel looked back to the fire. "Sometimes I suspect you of madness."

"'Madness'?" Aillas considered the word. "How so?"

"There would seem no other reason for your hatred of me."

Aillas laughed. "I feel no such hatred." He drank from the wine-sack. "Tonight I am kindly disposed; in fact, I see that I owe you a debt of gratitude."

"That debt is easily paid. You may give me a horse and let me go my way—"

"In this wild country? I would be doing you no favor. My gratitude, moreover, is indirect. You have earned it despite yourself."

Tatzel muttered: "Again the madness comes on you."

[…]"My remarks are probably somewhat opaque. I will explain. At Castle Sank I became enamored of a certain Tatzel, who in some respects resembled you, but who was essentially an imaginary creature. This phantom which lived in my mind possessed qualities which I thought must be innate to a creature of such grace and intelligence.

"Ah well, I escaped from Sank and went my way, encumbered still with this phantom, which now only served to distort my perceptions. At last I returned to South Ulfland.

"Almost by chance my most far-fetched daydreams were realized, and I was able to capture you: the real Tatzel. So then— what of the phantom?" Aillas paused to drink, tilting the wine-sack high. "This impossibly delightful creature is gone, and now is even hard to remember. Tatzel exists, of course, and she has freed me from the tyranny of my imagination, and here is the source of my gratitude."

The crucial scene, the apogee of the romance, the moment when Aillas and Tatzel come as close as possible to a meeting of souls then follows:

She spoke with fervor: "You are so wonderfully wrong-headed I can almost find it within myself to laugh at you! After chasing me across the moors, breaking my leg and causing me a dozen humiliations, you expect me to come creeping to you with adoration in my eyes, happy to be your slave, soliciting your caress, hoping with all my heart that I may compare favorably with your erotic daydream. You profess to find the Ska lacking in pathos, but your conduct toward me is absolutely self-serving! And now you sulk because I do not come sobbing to you and begging for your indulgence. Is it not a farce?"

Aillas heaved a deep sigh. "Everything you say is true. In all justice, I must admit as much. I have been driven by romantic passions to act out a dream."

Vance flatters and gratifies no one. But the human underpinnings of the scene are true to life.

THE THIRD OF MAY 1808 *by Francisco Goya, 1814, Museo del Prado, Madrid.*

MALEDICTA

Lester Glover

Among the sights Pony says he saw on his last walk in the woods are the Turks knocking the heads off the rest of the patrol. "They kneeled in sopping jacque," says Pony, "Divested of their mail." We're working our way to the mill trace on a night of little moon. News of the surrender has already riled the wives and mothers. Behind us rises their wailing. "Then they stepped out of their shoes," says Pony, "It was as if they expecting no particular mercy. They kneeled in the mud." Among the things Pony does not say is how he avoided the same fate. "You ask me, Kuntz, they knew they were going to get it in the neck." I and Pony whisper stories in the dark to keep from becoming too worried, too lonely. We are not ramblers, Pony and I. We are always around, gathered to wherever there is opportunity of warmth, always well within earshot of the walls. Stories are how we measure the dark distance between us.

"The levy, their sergeants dead or fled, were already beyond worldly cares," says Pony, "I was near enough to smell them in my bush. So I noted where the heads—eyes wide with blank despair—dropped into the mill trace," says Pony. "Let us now keep to whispers, Kuntz. Let us look for the stone I placed to mark the spot. Just up the hill from here, I hear the shoe thieves skulking through the gore. Nor would it surprise me were there still a stray Turk about."

"How ever did you survive?" I whisper. Pony's evasions vary amusingly.

"Simple, Kuntz," says Pony, "The Turks, as expert soldiers do, allowed me, the leader, the brave scout, through their line. I was at liberty to circle back once the killing began."

The moon is in the treetops. We are beneath the limit of this meager light. Pony must have struck some filthy deal with his would-be captor, perhaps the weakest of the bunch, posted toward the rear to catch escapees. Our progress along the bank is submerged under heavy bands of fog rising off the Pegnetz. I am feeling my way with my feet. I want to find where the stones change for the spillway dam. I wear my boots about my neck with Pony holding to my laces. He pulls me about randomly. I stop. "Your efforts to direct me through the fog are as useless as they are annoying," I say, "May we begin again? Attach yourself to my belt. Currently, you threaten me with strangulation."

"Force of habit," says Pony, desisting, "Forgive me." He speaks loudly again. I do not think he fears any shoe thieves. "Our patrol would have greatly benefited from your polite forbearance," says Pony, "Were it not for the sins burned into your face, you might have answered the sergeants' cry and therefore raised an earlier alarm to the presence of the Turk." I have little fear that there are still Mohammedans about, but I do not want to disturb the family of ducks that often roosts in the middle of the path. Pony grows lachrymose. "Before the end, they found themselves on their knees, murmuring the Latin of old habit, each crouched as if drawing a private chapel about himself." We begin to cross the spillway, a great coolness to either side. "I guess the moment meant to them nothing more than a little rest, another breath of life." Pony clicks his teeth in pained remembrance of his comrades. "The Turks drew them up by their hair most cruelly for the blade. The heads of Joacim the boxmaker, Thomas the wheelwright, and mason Konrad lie waiting to be discovered in the mire." We are to the opposite bank. "I saw the boxmaker bolt from the trees wheeling his arms like a running child, well beyond his senses. I had a vision of his next moments before they unfolded. As he sought the water, the change in the grade disordered his stride. The gentle Joacim tumbled and did not rise again until a tall Turk strode over and hauled him up by his hair. I saw all this from my bush." Something plops into the mill trace. A fish turning over.

"Kuntz, please pardon me," says Pony, "I am again distracting you from your effort to find the tell-tale stone. I will now hold to your belt in silence." I pat my foot around in the fog to reassure him. I go into the tall grass on a guess as to where the spillway begins. "Kuntz, you lead the way," says Pony with unwarranted confidence. "Now let us both be still."

With Pony's hand hooked into my belt. Any error of mine spills us both. Soon Pony cannot suppress himself. He startles me with his noise. At first I thought it was a duck taking flight. "Nobody got up to any noble work. There were no last words that would carry across the water. No backward glances to reassure a comrade. We were not soldiers. We will discover them with their eyes screwed shut. For who could face into the certain flash of the scimitar? Maybe Konrad. Maybe Konrad could."

"Maybe Konrad did." I spoke to reassure Pony but it seems to have had the opposite effect. He tugs hard at my belt. "We will soon see, Pony."

The fog clears a bit but the moon has disappeared, leaving us equally benighted. "What would you have them do, Kuntz?" asks Pony. "They were without sergeants." The black machinery of the mill freewheels behind us. We go up the trace, past the fish trap. There are indeed now lanterns lacing their way through the wood line like so many firebugs. Perhaps the shoe thieves are not just another legend.

"No noble work at all," says Pony. "No good word. Not a curse. This troubles me still."

Then we find the spot. Pony removes his gory robe, his own flapping shoes, hangs it all in the rattling branches. "I mean, are we not made the same way? Yet we seem to survive without masters." Pony draws a sharp breath when his feet hit the water.

"None of those named were called Kuntz," I say to Pony.

"Your father," begins Pony in a tightly constrained voice.

"Kuntz the wire drawer?" I supply. Pony often confuses the members of my numerous family.

"Attending to his business," he says, paraphrasing my father's motto. Pony submerges himself to the neck and then stands, now accustomed to the chill. "Your father was not present. Kuntz, I must admire the agility of your clan whenever the Lion comes around to raise a patrol," he says.

"Silver crosses many palms *intra muros*," I say to the nude Pony, now standing on a sandbar. His sex has shrunken to a tight bud. "What would you have had the unfortunate prisoners do? Struggle? Weep?" The harsh whispers of the thieves up the hill reach down to us, words like blades drawn across a strop.

"Imagine no lack of tears among the levy, Kuntz," says Pony. "The rabble are always given to histrionics." He wades out in the current, sweeping his legs abut in wide, searching arcs. "Our patrol melted like women. Those too dazed to kneel wandered away to rave. These maddened rovers held in their intestines, become like women with aprons full of parsnips. They sought private and dignified departure but instead served as sport for the older Turks who strung their bows. The gutted, half-alive Christians went about laughing like brooks, chirping their last when the black arrows sprouted from their backs." The water has risen to Pony's balls. His search is drawing him farther up the trace. "Kuntz, can you still make me out in the dark?" His steps are ginger, yet made slow by the reservoir sludge. He gets the words out in short runs. "Mark where I am, for a meaty stone ebbs at my shins and now I must go under to the slime," he says. Perhaps to encourage himself Pony says, "I walked about them as we do when shamming beggars." Pony draws a great breath, submerges himself. I hope he will opt for silence when he surfaces. A bottom fish turns over, disturbed from its mud.

"Hush Pony," I say, to nobody.

"Behold Konrad," says Pony, bursting forth from the mire. "Say hello to Kuntz." Pony flings the mason's heavy head by its hair. It thuds down on the bank, the first of many I won't catch. I stop it from rolling back in with my foot. "Forward my regards to the dame mason," says Pony. I feel bad so I straighten the remnant. It is not Konrad, the eyes squared to a chalk line. Nevertheless, I fix its gaze homeward. I line them all up so they look out over the river toward the barbican lantern. Konrad's head recalls the shape of the solid, flat molars I prise from its jaw. Everyone else's head bears little resemblence to the teeth found within. In life Konrad's stern gaze seemed itself the negative of the lozenges he struck into ashlar stones. In all forms can be divined a rightness. The last face Konrad makes betrays a strange stupid, wide-eyed surprise.

The next morning, we're at the octroi trying to warm ourselves around the schlepper's bonfire. Pony is sitting, face out to the market traffic. He still has the shakes from his midnight bath, so when he puts one hand out the other to his heart—a gesture he says granted him safe passage through a foreign land—he is more convincing than usual. We're three pfennigs to the good already.

"Pony," I say, "I have my secrets, too." Pony scurries out into the roadway for a carrot. Any stray legumes fallen from the car when they mount the bridge are fair game. "You know, you aren't the only one who has seen things." He snaps the carrot but also throws my share into the schlepper's stew. "Pray," Pony asks, "what have you seen, Kuntz? Of what hidden afflictions do you suffer?" He pulls at my coat. "What secrets voyage within this artless dodger?"

"Karl the file cutter filed his incisors," I say, instead of what I was saving up. I always fall back on whatever happens to be in my pocket when Pony pulls at my tunic. Besides it was true. "As I speak, the serpent darts of these very teeth click about in my palm."

"Kuntz you know nothing of the sort. Your world is tightly circumscribed by your own fables. Everything you see is seen through one eye, begrudgingly half open. A parochial eye, at that." Pony begins crunching at his carrot. I admit his abuse warmed me a little.

"I'll tell you what I have seen," I say, standing, "I have seen Karl's wife turn her back to you and lift her skirts." I'm not certain he can hear me over the carrot. The schleppers and the whores who congregate in the shadow of the octroi whoop it up a bit. Once the sun takes a turn they will continue to shuffle along in the tower's shade in the hope that, by avoiding full light, they will be exempt from the ban. People are wont to make up whatever they fancy about the ban. Which is one reason why they aren't happy to see my face. "Whatever story with which you plied Karl's wife certainly has stuck," I say to Pony, earning the silence of the schleppers suddenly tuned to any whisper. "Was it the Tale of the Seven Cities which did the trick?"

Pony produces a spasm of outrage beginning at his shoulders which draws him up from his beggar's crouch. "Mitzi cares not who oversees her passions, Kuntz." Now out comes his empty palm, still shaking with the Pegnetz's chill. His body crumples as his feigned outrage suddenly melts to solicitude, earning him a pfennig from a passing hookmaker, his wares hung upon his shoulder. The man murmurs a blessing or worse, takes his distance, pulling along his hare-lipped apprentice.

"Joacim the box maker's eyeteeth are pristine," I say. "I have examined them closely, but can discover no flaw. They are no worse for having spent two summers on campaign. Very strange." But Pony isn't listening. He is instead engaging his next mark, employing a sidling step which makes even me look away in embarrassment, fearful that I become infected by his physical indignity. Confronted with all this, the peasant's wife merely spits. Pony makes an indignant pirouette.

"Return them to the sack with the others, Kuntz. Nothing is now pristine. The woods are thick with Turks and sudden arrows. Degeneration has become general and value is bound only to the market-day beholder." Pony shakes his finger at the woods. "One day they will come in number, the Turks. The ban already gives them no pause. The lantern will be tipped over and the barbican will burn. This menace explains, partly, why the women have become so loose."

Pony tests the hookmaker's coin. The token crumbles in his jaws. He spits out the pot metal which splatters black onto the stocking of a shocked foreigner. The foreigner abuses him in foreign, fixing a shamming Pony to the spot by the force of surprisingly harsh consonants. Serbian, I believe. At the end of this toxic apostrophe, he rewards Pony with a great clout, which the latter had been japing to avoid. Pony's scraping and bowing would normally have saved him from further abuse, but the foreigner has packed harsher custom in his baggage.

"Many strange folk about on the roads," Pony groans. "I fear the building of some great migration from Croatia." He pats his swollen eye and crawls back into his crouch, catches sight of something mysterious and distant, lowers his head. I know the look.

"We owe no honor to those who do not issue from within our walls," I say.

"There stands the jester," says Pony dejectedly, running his fingers between the cobbles, searching.

And indeed there he is, hulking about in his jester's armor, somehow resplendent in spite of the leaden sun. For me, it is too late. I catch the glare of the dual brass disks which serve as eyes. Doubtlessly, the jester has likewise seen my face flash up at him. I—and perhaps Pony—are now selected for his justice. Our best hope is that some greater crime than loitering distract him.

"Everything the devil does enjoys the sanction of the Almighty," mutters Pony. "Every man a murderer." Nobody has ever heard the jester speak. This principle, this anticipation of his judgement, underpins the ban. We don't even discuss the jester's silence. One of the schleppers looks up with a bright anger in his face seemingly drawn directly from the fire that warms us all. My comrade seems certain to suffer further blows. But the whores slowly draw the schleppers off into the shadows, leaving the stew to simmer.

"Speaking that way will draw him down," hisses a farm boy yoked with muscle at Pony. Shy of the women, he sounds more concerned than aroused.

"You will have your time," I say to the drudge. "Regain your stool or bring your friends." The boy has made no such threat. I just want to clear the air.

"Evil rushes in to serve as proxy for the good," says Pony. "We will all have our time."

All of us are convinced that the jester sees far but, beyond that commonplace, strange ideas abound. There is no agreement as to how far he might *hear*, whether he is deafened or sharpened by his grotesque horned helmet.

"It is said the Jester's visor rises on emptiness," quavers the massive boy.

"The armored getup is an obvious disguise for our lord," says Pony. "Who merely wishes to displace assassins toward his body double."

"His innards spin and tick with demonic clockwork," says a famished curl of a man, ladling stew into a bowl.

"Indeed," says Pony, waving away the subject. "Now let us all be still. A procession hearkens to the Lion's drum." A lazy, dry beat resounds in the streets beyond the octroi. Of the jester there is now no sign.

"The citizens gather to beg divine mercy," says Pony. "I have been abused by a foreigner, perhaps an Alsatian or a Pole, who now passes gaily within the walls. This is maybe the big day. How much longer am I to be detained?"

"Who knows?," I say. "But this being a market day, I rather suspect the Lion is merely drumming up the audience for an execution."

Toward our fire, comes no murmur or wail of deranged prayer. No such noise as that which rises when the sinful excesses of the citizenry have become too weighty for the walls to contain them. For sure, the impacted evils of the city result in a kind of ambient heat. Hives bloom across every face. The sign of civilization is a rougeole spread by the daylight whores. It comes as a twitch or tic with no obvious source, a persistent itch between the shoulder blades. Whatever form the malediction adopts, it can only be evaded by taking refuge in the countryside temporarily.

"We needn't move, boys," I say. More of the peasant lads are standing up, shifting around. They know well the smell of blood. "We have heard this drum many times. It is beaten by the Lion who is distracted by giving directions to his sergeants. These constables now part the crowds so the handcart of the condemned may cross the bridge. The drum is only meant to stir the humors of the idle." The daylight whores flee the shadow of the barbican in one nervous moment, arranging their clothes, making themselves as respectable as they can before crossing into the light. Half the faces around the schlepper's fire have never witnessed a hanging. The farm boy does not suspect to what degree a wild joy overcomes the throng after the unpleasantness is concluded. It far exceeds a hog killing.

This day, no priest in a feathered cap leads the penitent in prayer. This day, there are no penitent. There, a couple accused of concocting potions are lashed to rude chairs, that are in turn lashed to a handcart seconded from a gong farmer. The notion of a riot rises from behind, threatening to overwhelm the rank of sergeants in the train of the cortege. A flock of waifs pelt over the cobbles, free as air driven by the tide. They hurtle down the promenade, winding through the barren sycamores like swallows. The orphans mount the rail around the gallows, briefly disturbing the crows that had gathered to pick at the old bones suspended. The crowd floods the spaces to this same rail. The Lionreads the charges. A sort of dual fornication. The sense of them is hard to follow or imagine. So one naturally imagines the worst, most secret desires. There is no room around the rock or between the trees, going back all the way to the wall. The crowd groans and titters.

How our world diminishes over this chill season. Time itself attenuates. The woods we all know thicken with murder. News of islands in the south seas falling to the Turk trouble even the schleppers who only navigate oxcarts by single memories. You get the feeling that affairs, now undone, will never return as before. Your world, ours, sends no notice when it so diminishes. You always find out the hard way, come up on its hard limits. Right now the world has diminished to the circle of our fire and might further shrink to the circumference of the cauldron where bubbles our stew. One of the farm boys says he will renounce his bond this winter. Of the rumored rebel army he says, "It is lead by no bishop or prince."

"It is led by an arsonist," says Pony. "The ranks of the bandits form behind the simple standard of a peasant's boot hung from a string."

"What luscious power," says the boy's sullen mate, considering his own shabby boots. Vendors ladle out hot cider at the limit of the scrum. A pair of fools provide a confusing alternative for the squeamish. They sitting astride a sawhorse, facing each other within arm's reach, each taking a turn at bashing the other in the head with the warming pan they pass to the other after each blow.

"By all means," encourages Pony, "You should depart this very morning." My friend is about to speak Godspeed to the drudges, but a bell is rung, drawing away our attention.

The golden crown the widow Wörner wore owed to a single golden braid woven into itself. Who had attended to her that morning? The braid does not fall when the hangman removes the pins, for it is held in place by a spell. The Lion, already hoarse from all his previous roaring, reads the charges.

"That the widow Wörner confused and strangled her guests, bewildering them by the service of a toxic postprandial; that the widow Wörner then summoned incapacitating demons which took of her guests' flesh; that she herself did so join in the supper; that she falsely claimed to be with child upon her confession of the previous crimes. Her health, while seated, is sufficient for the sentence."

"They are to hang her in her chair?" says the oldest schlepper rubbing his hands together, "This I have never seen before."

Sometimes, in memory, the image of the widow Wörmer is joined by her accomplice, a barrel chested warlock with the apparent constitution of a horse. He, too, remains seated in a rickety chair that barely sustains his weight. I am vexed with this impossible image of a seated horse. For love nor money, there now seems little place for anyone else but one's closest brother. Pony and I are too burnt and seedy to pass for beggar waifs. We take in as much as we can without moving. We stick to shadow. "Have you never really seen the next valley?" asks Pony. "I have seen Bruges, Paris, and the estuary of the Thames." We sit at the schleppers' fire, a penny shy of paying our way over bridge. It would be only a short stroll.

That night I follow Pony away from the silver tinkling of the remaining coals of the schleppers' dying fire. We shuffle up to the barbican together.

"We'll be kicked away again," I say.

"This time, Kuntz, everything will be different," says Pony. "My walk makes me invisible to minor authority and the more fortunate. Allow me to demonstrate how I can summon the guardsmen's gaze and yet divert it in nearly the same moment. He will take me in and then fear that by doing so that his fate and mine are the same. Witness my stoop, correct me if the music of my movement becomes too impossible."

We go up the way. "I admit, Pony," I say, "You do appear as if you are retaining your intestines. You do not have the look of a survivor. No, you have the bizarre allure of a deserter from the fight who has been badly brained or spined. You seem to be seeking final grace at a too-distant altar." I address the latecomers heading to the platform. I am worried about the jester, but shy of looking to the parapet. "Here beside me walks one of widow Wörner's poisoned guests." Pony now stiffens his knees and swings his legs from the hips. "Pony," I say, "You have outdone yourself." There can be no deviation from the gate now. We are almost within earshot.

"I appreciate all that, Kuntz," says Pony. "I have been thinking about this all day while you have cozied yourself to the fire."

"Every word I say is always sincere," I say, "Although I remain convinced that the price of losing our place at the fire will be more kicks."

This time the bastards quit crossing their halberds. Pony holds to me, continuing the new sham. I push my bonnet down low to my brow and put my hands to my cheeks to better warm them. "We are now just a pair of tinkers," mutters Pony. The market concluded, the square beyond the bridge gate stands forlorn. In the end, they don't even ask to see the color of our money.

"Who gives a damn what you are?" says one of the bastards, too old for the duty, too old to take a step. "Who asked you to speak?"

"I, for one, do not give a damn," says the other bastard, who is my second-cousin Karl Kuntz, wearing the tin hat of which he is so fond. He must have lost at throws to be on night watch. "And I did not ask you lot to speak," he concludes. There is no generosity in his soul.

"I see you Karl Kuntz," I say just before I absorb his kick. Which stays him not at all from giving me another. "I have knowledge of your shameful losses," I add. My implied threat stays him from a third attack.

"Oh, let it go," says Karl Kuntz with a defeated air, "Just as I have let go you and your gooseberry."

Pony takes me by the arm before Karl Kuntz can complete his weary progress toward the corner where stands his halberd.

"Let us away to wake the Jew in his hole," says Pony.

"To the Goosefoot," I say.

At the Goosefoot, everyone shuffles off the way they do when a gong farmer turns down their street. At the Goosefoot, everyone stands aside from everyone else because everyone who drinks at the Goosefoot is a gong farmer. Within, the patorns are arranged in a sort of equilibrium of spacing owing to the pressure raised by their funk. At this hour, the sky beginning to kindle, there is always a newly-stained farmer coming in, just having finished dumping his cart into the vile pool which festers beyond the powder works. You can feel the pressure rising. Pony and I have no intention of lingering.

"The Jew hole," growls Pony to Big Kurtz. Big Kurtz makes a sign that travels all the way across the low, grumbling room to Little Gross. Little Gross snaps out of his stupor, leaps up, and creaks open the cellar door with great effort. Pony pauses to consider his own path through the greasy gong farmers hunched, spaced evenly to tabletops sloppy with ale. He puts his arm across my chest just before I sneeze. "Kuntz, observe these humble laborers at their ease, their woes now discarded like a bad hand. Their rounded back bear the foul stains incurred in the course of their travails. See how the dame in the corner pulls upon her mustache. The burden of the lugubrious ambiance grows. For now, she recalls olden loves in Arcadian glades. Now, protected by a life circumscribed by the city wall, shored up by the strictures of a strange ban, the jester's oversight, and the common destiny of the whore, even the dank air rising from the Jew hole must carry with it some note of liberty."

"If only briefly, Pony," I allowed. "The bulk of her custom has yet to descend. The building pressure you remark will find sole issue once we draw the cellar door closed behind us. The trollup will soon be drawing the curtain on her love alcove."

"Darkness makes her again a maiden," says Pony, dismissing the scene with a wave in parting. The gamblers just set down to a game, one of whom was separating the banned faces from the deck, adjust themselves away from us. Little Gross stands aside.

We pass through the door. "It would be no surprise if some day soon we pulled gong paddles alongside them ourselves," I say. Guttering lamps in niches light our way down. A warm gust chases us down a ways.

"Or else a Venetian oar," supplies Pony, forever dreaming his way around the next bend, rise, or wave.

"Change is the only constant," I agree. Pony removes the last lamp to carry with us. He steps carefully so as not to upset the fuel. "I will light our way forward from behind," he says, gesturing me forward. I can vaguely feel the flame's warmth following on my shoulder. I cannot keep myself from backward glances. Per usual, Pony comforts, shushes, urges me onward. We go on this way for quite a distance. I lose count of my paces. We go even farther. The Jew hole is turns out to be a long tunnel. It once thrived with Jews. Or so it is said. The place is really like a street, a long corridor of flagstones and foundations with many rough lintels and recesses. Perhaps it was once a street, since paved over. It is difficult to reckon, but I am convinced we are somewhere beyond the barbican.

"The scale of this warren is quite unexpected," I say.

"It is said the Jew hole connects to the basements of Byzantium itself," says Pony. Apropos of nothing he says, "One always wonders, Kuntz, just how much of life is determined by the misasma that rises from underground." We wade a clear stream teeming with blind fish. Is this seepage, the underground shadow of the Pegnetz? Pony goes before me, sets the lamp down on the far shore, climbs the rubble of a stair and knocks at the door with a gleaming charm nailed to the jamb. The fish set themselves to a frenzy of dull jaws against my legs but cannot feed. Madov has come to occupy the portico above as I wade out. He gathers his gabardine around him with the put-out air of a woman too long in attendance of her suitor's arrival. I am shocked to see the Jew shod in the sort of pointy shoes long-ago proscribed by the ban. Lamentable, this mental guardsman of mine.

Madov neither greets us nor invites us within. "Do not trespass the threshold lest your odor invade my cheeses," he says.

"So you choose to begin our negotiations by shorting Kuntz and me common hospitality," says Pony. "I cannot confess surprise. Nevertheless, we will make no complaint about our wet stockings here in your cold cellar."

Madov takes us in over his heavy spectacles. "Nevertheless," he says. He turns and drags a bench across the the door with difficulty, raising a great clamor which animates dark, distant movement deeper in the Jew hole. He gives one one end of the bench a final weak push and, gestures. Is Madov the only one, I wonder. The last of his kind?

"Sit," says Madov.

"Sit," Pony says to me, as it is I who carry the teeth. I sit just within the gust of Madov's cheesy breath. Pony puts his back to mine. "It is to you Kuntz, my factor, to negotiate," says Pony. "Whereas I will draw my dirk and face out to whatever slinking danger surely nears." Madov strops a knife across the sole of his pointed slipper. In the poor light he produces what I first take to be an apple. He pares away the rind. The fruit releases a perfume, astringent and sweet, which immediately cancels the rotten bouquet emanating from Madov's den. The rustling in the dark seems too copious and heavy to be rat feet. Neat sections of the pale, tart flesh disappear into his beard.

"So?" says Madov with his mouth full, "What have you now?" I untie our toothy purse, leaving it to my side more. Madov has to stop chewing, grunt, lean his large body toward me. This way I can see beyond the portico.

There, the verdigris husks of his cheeses dangle in the candlelight, turning in the drafts. Who brought them down? How long ago? There comes across the floor further intense bursts of small movement that my eye cannot quite follow. Small cones of paper hang midway along the length of each cheese's string. I suppose this is to keep the rats from feasting. Below the cheeses, Madov's tables glint with split sacks of ducats still otherwise secured with a noble seal. Golden eyes blaze out from beneath an fantastic armoire. I worry that they might not be those of a cat. Am fleetingly reminded of the jester, though his presence here is impossible.

"They're local," says Pony into the dark, meaning our sack of teeth which Madov has now retrieved and is poking through. "Not yet a week old," says Pony. "Some may yet be alive." I am struck by further sights from within Madov's rooms. Beside a pyramid of strange spiky fruit, stands the jester remade in miniature. A trick of eyesight or the effect of fouled air. Nevertheless, I have the impression it has just marched into view, stiff-legged across the length of table, having drawn to a halt and turned toward me. I close my eyes to dispell the apparition and shake my head until I see stars. A cloud of erratic amber points gathers around an indeterminate center then wheels in the manner of sparrows, and disperses. Such gloom has swallowed us. I realize my eyes are open and that the golden scatter can only be our last delivery for Madov: the bell jar of fireflies Pony and I collected while traipsing through the upper meadows in high summer. I wonder what sustaining nectar Madov concocts that they remain quick.

"Something struggles beneath your surface," says Madov without looking away from the heavy sack. "You abuse yourself from within." Madov looks upon me fully. "Your mind is a drowning pool." I look to him and smile witht he smile which always charms my father. All news of what goes on within our walls travels leaden conduits, until is pours over the hairy porches of Madov's ears. I know better than to trade metaphors with people who laugh at me from behind a screen. Already he knows the answer. Already he knows that Pony must depart. The Jew lights a taper between us, goes back to sorting through the teeth in the gloom, flicking away the broken and the rotten, among them Karl's finely pointed incisors. Madov presses each piece into the meat of his thumb.

"Today was market day," says Madov. He sounds unsure. Perhaps he is testing. How does he mark time? Madov carries with him the air of a wealthy, yet embattled person, always in need of confirmation.

"Today was market day," agrees Pony emphatically.

"And there was an execution?" asks Madov plaintively, as if afraid to be disappointed.

"There were three," says Pony. "But came a drizzle. So there was only poor custom, muted mirth, and shortened confessions."

"What foreigners did you spot?" he asks.

"No foreigners," says Pony, "None from the east, anyway."

"Suspensions?" asks Madov, warming. "Characterize the magnitude of delight the rope inspired among the onlookers."

"Only a single suspension," says Pony. "Only the usual delight. The urchins climbed the rail and the watch did not impede them from riding the poor sinner's legs."

"Dear children are the vessels of small mercies," says Madov, "What was the condemned's transgression?"

"A horse thief and evader of the ban," says Pony, "Caught on the wrong side of the octroi. The Lion read out an additional list of delinquencies, including many nights skulking and cutting the tresses of girls while they slept in bed."

"How was the body clothed?" asks Madov quietly.

"As befits a boy of thirteen," I take up. "You need only dare to leave your hole to see for yourself." Madov draws up straight, stares down his nose at me. I take my eye off of the finely-wrought homunculus on the table. I feel Pony at my back as he wheels about at some noise. "The hanged lad was vested in immaculate linen," I say. The table is empty where the homonculus stood.

"Purest white," adds Pony nervously, "Soon enough stained beyond recovery. But why rely on our shifty report, Madov? Why not render yourself to the spectacle upon hearing the drum? Bring along your wooden bowl and have a few warm chestnuts? We would never betray your disguise."

Madov has now finished selecting the teeth he needs. He arranges them on the bench carefully.

"Retrieval of the youth's vestments would be met with great reward," mutters Madov. He seems to lack any conviction that we might recover them from the hangman, is perhaps thinking of yet another more capable team of miscreants.

"To answer you question, masters," says Madov, "I have grown weary of nearly any surface spectacle." The Jew matches eyeteeth, holding them up for inspection. "I have seen it all before." He pushes molars to molars with his bony fingers, incisors to incisors. "The drum, for example. The beating is a political fiction. The crowds already know the place and time. They have their calendars marked but nevertheless pretend to be stirred by the Lion. The break out their feathers and silk and gather to the gibbet like so many crows nesting in the shadow of the cathedral."

Madov spreads out the gold.

"The best I can do," he says, with no hint of apology.

I reflect that I have seen Madov flick away an unknown number of our hard-won teeth into the dark. But past congress with him has shown it is equal to accepting a stroll down a one-way alley. Anyone else, I would make him pay for the waste.

"When have you ever refused?" he reminds Pony, needlessly. "Is there to be an exception this time?"

The taper gutters. The pressures in the aether change. The Goosefoot's cellar door, or that of some other entryway, must have come open. All Madov would have to do is lower a spancel over our shoulders like a warming stole. Pony and I could end up joined to each other for eternity in one sorcerous gesture.

Madov groans and regains his feet. The negotiation over, his mood seems to have improved.

"Are you beginning to suspect me of a conjury, young Kuntz?" asks Madov, smiling gently.

Pony spits into the darkness. "Why can I not stand?" he says, "I am hissing with ire! Kuntz, will you please rise?" Now, it seems his ire extends to me.

"Pony, I see no spancel or band."

"I have employed some sympathetic magic," says Madov. "I set the moment's echo in a sort of ephemeral plaster. A strong lad like you could quite easily overcome such tricks." Madov is not addressing Pony. "You need only whistle."

"Who approaches?" I ask. Madov scoops his teeth into the empty purse, rises from the bench, steps backward into his charmed doorway. I might have made a schelpper weren't it for my inability to raise a sharp note. No beast would obey me.

"Tell me of the hangman's favor today," says Madov.

I elbow Pony until he tells it. Something stubborn in me keeps me from speaking.

"Though their crimes were well beyond the repeated indiscretion of the simple horse thief who preceded them," says Pony, "The widow and her warlock were spared the rope."

"And so the city is unburdened of another pair of fornicators," says Madov.

"At the very least. But at cost to common faith in competent justice. Schmidt botched his stroke," put in Pony with disgust. "With grim result. You see, he attempted both heads at once. Set them back to back as you have done to us: I, the licentious warlock, to Kuntz's loose widow. The warlock was a man of great charm and appetite."

"I resent that, Pony," I say.

"The widow," Pony continues, "administered her recipes to their guests. Among them was an ingenue. Once the poison was fast within the girl's extremities she set to a dance. Upon her exhaustion both partook of her body. Yet she lived. The jester led her out by the hand to witness his justice. She stood before us, a ruined spectacle in rusty bandages."

"She will enter an immured order?" asks Madov, clucking his tongue. "Of course she will," he said in answer to his own question. "Her dowry in ruin. What waste."

Pony continues. "The fiendish pair refuse the fortifying draught offered by the hang-man. Perhaps they are immune to intoxicants. Schmidt, for his part, takes a long stoop such as we have never seen him do before. Perhaps the draught's effect is why his backswing wavers, his stance slightly overbalanced, before his cut trammels their cheeks most unjustly. Whereas the crowd had cheered the demise of the previous scapegoat, were gleeful at encouraging the children to leap for his belt and thus ride him down, the most dire groan now arose. Another stroke, one poorly prepared in haste, was necessary to end the noise."

Madov adjusts his spectacles. "What revolting butchery," he says. The teeth remain before me, four neat arcs of good, if not perfect, dentition. Enough for two sets of choppers for our lord.

"Something nears," whimpers Pony. His back wiggles against mine.

"I shall finish the account as I fear my brother Pony now pants with fear and exhaustion," I say. "The worst was yet to come. After the first wayward stroke, the Lion posed himself beneath the pair, gripping to their common restraint, heedless of the curtains of blood. At first, it looked as he intending some lewd congress, but he used his own weight to steady them in their chairs, just as a framer employs a windlass. Alas, his hands were drawn into the path of the blade by the witch's final spasm."

"Do you see what you're missing, Madov?" says Pony laconically. For my part, I have the idea that Madov misses very little of what happens within our walls on any level. Maybe even less without.

"Tell me, Kuntz," says Madov, "Who recovered the Lion's hands? By what means? And were wooden implements employed?"

"The jester strode forward and recovered them while they were binding the Lion."

"Recovered?" says Madov, "From the rock? Or did they chance to fall upon the Lion's body as he lay? Does the Lion yet live?" Madov scowls with disappointment when I shake my head at his questions. "What of Kuntz Bauer?" asks Madov, becoming conspiratorial. "The thief of tresses," he adds, "And your cousin." Behind me, Pony is increasing his struggle to move. His whistle is low and weak, but building.

"He is so far removed from us," I say.

"Your cousin a wire drawer as well as a horse thief," said Madov, conspirationally. "And your father's apprentice."

"I'm not going to argue the point," I say, "His mother is French."

"A story that should hold for another day or two," says Madov, "This much for the lot." He pushes more four crown across the bench. Then he pushes a fifth. This piece makes no noise on the wood. "And one more to divide among you for the trouble." He could have just rocked his cheese knife over our sovereign's golden profile, split him into equal share. But he does not take that small trouble. He has paid us more for the story than the teeth.

"What charge do you make us?" says Pony.

"What do you want us to do?" I say.

"I release you both to rise," says Madov, making circles in opposing directions with his bent hands.

My eyes are now at one with the murk. I've become used to the diverse stinks. A part of me resolves to abiding in this place. Against a background of the most somber corner of the Madov's rooms, I glimpse over Madov's shoulder, hanging from a bent horseshoe, a garland of golden tresses.

"Kuntz, I fear we have taken a fell detour on our way back to the Goosefoot," says Pony, when the taper Madov gave us finally dies.

"What of all these unsettling arrangements of remains we have passed, the knobby layers of hollow pates, the legions of shank bones laid in chevrons? While distracted by this grim ossuary did you fail to note the abandoned machinery? The forlorn winch? Did you feature a sort of driving shaft articulated to facilitate further descent, the parasitic shafts and rambles? The mole machine? These are signs of black industry about, to which some hero should attend."

"I have forsaken any hope that we emerge at the Goosefoot, Pony," I say. I wonder if Pony, at that moment in the dark, would believe me were I to suggest we would soon be warmed by a Byzantine sun or scale the mountains of the moon. I might say anything and be believed. Instead, I say "Some disorientation is the price of keeping our path separate from that which follows in our traces." I have kept from Pony my recent visions of Madov's spoils, including the armored homunculus which japed me from the Jew's table. Presently, we get to a rising place of newer air, which later becomes a watery shaft with iron rungs nailed into its walls. I have to point it out to a despairing Pony to keep him moving. He seems drawn backward toward the abandoned machines. "My hand has found a rung," I say.

"We did not descend this stair," says Pony. "This shaft continues below." My counterpart now sounds near to weeping. "My foot pivots upon the precipice." His voice is tinged with the same powerlessness which suffused his description the recent Turkish massacre. "We are chased well beyond the Jew hole, Kuntz," he sighs.

"We are certainly beyond the hole and the walls," I say, "But the ban, like all words, like crows, follows one everywhere. Let us take what strenght we can in this truth. I have detected no change in the pressure of the maledicta written into my face. And there is light above. And the rungs are set regularly. My hand alights upon the second."

"Mind how you go, Kuntz," says Pony, rallying some. "We occupy but a ledge." He kicks a pebble into the well. We listen to it click. "Perhaps we are meant to continue our descent," he adds in a forlorn tone. I find the proper rung before we hear the splash of Pony's shard. I can feel Pony's hand at my instep all the way up, so closely does he crowd me. In spite of my fear that he will grab at my leg for security and so tumble us both, we return to the surface.

"Now that we have emerged into good light, Kuntz," says Pony, "Show me the nine crowns."

"Be still, hale companion," I say in my softest voice, "Observe first our surroundings."

I suppose I'm expecting some renewed planet, but we have instead emerged from the rotten mouth of Grüble's disused well, the rotten heart of his ruined farm. "Murderers and demons have been burning the lands of the more distant families," I say, "We now find ourselves at a sort of way station." The hall and its low tower, its masonry lightly deranged, have been adopted by passing herders, road agents, and deserters. The hearth is damp and already young trees stand in Grüble's grown-out fields.

We poke our way in amid black timbers, deeper into the vestiges of the house. Within are stirrings and snores. "We walk among those lost to the best slumber of the day, that which comes just after morning," I say. "How delightful to be tucked-in, still just when the world begins to stir." I recognize a few of the daylight whores fled from yesterday or before. There are the schleppers who follow them, but also the sleeping forms of families mixed in. "Soon we will be kipped out alongside them, Pony. Find yourself a lonesome miss and spoon. Do not insist upon the division of our nine crowns at this moment, as it seems certain that some of these villains must be scamping woke. We are surely observed through the insincerely-lidded eyes of a born assassin."

"Show them me, now, Kuntz," hisses Pony, "Hold back none." Pony squeezes my arm until I twist myself away from his influence. But I do not otherwise resist his wishes. In the light which infiltrates through the shakes and slats, I show him the nine brilliant crowns. "This is what our work has come to," I say. Such sacrifice to buy our way back to the comfort which lies past the guard, where the ban is properly applied. Such sacrifice only to bed down in the hollow of the jester's mailed hand. The dispossessed cart their way toward our walls with no real knowledge of this price, stopping at Grüble's dead farm in vague hope that a day later they will arrive where justice is sharply dispensed. Campfire rumors of the jester interest them less than the rising cries of wolves.

"Take the nine crowns, Pony," I say, settling into the corner of what once had been the larder, down in the dust and mouse turds. "Together they make a handful. I do not want them. Without your aquatic efforts, who knows where we would be now. You alone braved the gar and the slime. I trust you to spend them to better our interest."

"Equity demands I press one coin upon you, Kuntz. One coin at least," says Pony, "Your actions were worthy of at least an apprentice barber." Pony's attentions are briefly drawn away by agitated murmur. A patched-up mercenary in ruined mail strikes out in his slumber. "A dream, brother," says another mercenary, comforting his companion. "Perhaps even better than the barber himself," allows Pony. In his palm, so only I might see, shines the crown.

"I won't have it, Pony," I say, feeling myself settle further into the floor, "Leave me to sleep a while."

"Very well, loyal Kuntz," says Pony kindly, "I know you have about you a tenth. We will divide it on the new day. Pray the piece has not been magicked to flee under the knife." I roll over, piqued. Pony chuckles, says he knows me like a brother.

"Hoo," says Pony, "Shush now."

That morning, in my best sleep, I dream of my father on his bench, drawing wire, trying to sell me on mastering his line of work. He diminishes an iron bar, pulling the metal through an eye made of some harder metal. He shunks off a piece from a corner of the bar, ever rotating it to the most prominent corner, working by feel, shimming in a smaller eye into the bench when the time comes. He wroks like this until he holds a length of wire. Only the ban keeps him from putting a crimp in it—wire delivered to the armorer must be only lightly coiled at most. It seems this dream land is also afflicted by Turks, as there is constant demand for links to knit new dream coats of mail.

In the way of dreams, I knew what he was going to say before he said it. "Son," says my dream father, "All you need in life is a turnip and a little slab of lard." His work is as immutable as his pronouncement. He makes the dull side shiny, the clumsy useful, the stocky tensile. Even in dreamland, condemned to the piggy ingots gathered about his bench, father spins no gold. Such sorcery is to the armorer, who stands up soldiers made of links. They rise from the dust to his hand with a jingle. My father's weary hands gather wire into coils before handing them to me. It is my job to hang the coils on the joinery, like the locks of some vanquished metal giant. Somehow, by the logic of dreams, I know this scene comes from the time before I followed Pony's cheery whistle out the gate, from the time when Pony rode a roan palfrey.

When I regain my senses, in the ruin of Grüble's farm again, I am listening to what villains remain abroad in the yard. They are rooting about for fallen apples like pigs, pelting each other with the rotten ones they find. "Just after midnight I rose to take my ease and saw two spirits rise from the very spot," says the patched-up mercenary to his mate. He looks beneath the cover we left standing open and admits that there is, indeed, a sort of stair beneath. Pony is still near to me, within reach, innocent as he dreams. His arms wrap himself in tight embrace, just as one leans forward to caress one's mount after a successful charge.

A month later, so much happens. After Pony dices away our nine crowns, I get us over by picking through market scraps and associated slops. I see the market crowds come, but mostly abandon their empty carts once their meager wares are exhausted. They set up camps beside the moat and along the Pegnetz. From this uncustomary disorder rises wood smoke. Soon there is a penury of wood. Drunken conversations wake the quality sleeping within the wall. Servants slam shutters on these refugees to no avail.

Pleading lines of peasants seeking admission to the hospital clog the octroi. Through it all, the jester becomes more outlandish. In addition to the brass disks, the helm entire grows, becomes crowned with the dorsal fin of a gar, the scales chased in brass or gold. The visor is now extruded to a point such that it resembles the muzzle of a fox. Pony and I watch the jester glimmer and clank past the embrasures from our spot on the trace where the turning machinery keeps ice from forming on the spillway.

"Surely this metamorphosis is the result of peculiar and sinful pursuits within the walls," says Pony. "I am powerless to speculate. The jester's bestial aspect seems dire augury. Witness the supplementary brass lenses now welded behind his head." Indeed, two bright points shine out from the rear of his helm.

"Pony, you are easily perplexed," I say. "The jester has simply put by a stock of astounding protections. An extravagant collection of helmets does not rise to augury of any sort. Do not allow your imagination to exercise your humor overly."

"Only one question really occupies me, Kuntz," says Pony. He means when will I produce the tenth coin he believes Madov slipped me. The sun can neither rise nor set without some pecuniary allusion. Together we contemplate the confluence of the hearth smoke from the noble quarter from a rise across the mill trace, where I have knocked together a sort of hut concealed within a bramble. Nothing will disabuse him of the suggestion of the final coin withheld. Pony says nothing, need say nothing, pretending instead to be lost in the majestic vision forming in the smoke.

In the pregnant silence I refuse to fill, I notice Karl Kuntz relieve the guard at the gate. Characteristically, he leans on his halberd and eats and apple. Cousin Karl has put on something of a gut. What a life. We could go back to his woman and brats at any time. I leave Pony in the thrall of the sooty Andalusian castles he sees forming above the chimney pots. I hasten to the barbican before the chill can bite Karl Kuntz. I shake my bag. "Keep your money," says Karl Kuntz. I rattle the small purse anyway. It is full of tinkling glass and has yet to fail at conjuring hospitality. "Come in, come in," says Karl Kuntz, putting aside his halberd. As a respecter of the ban, Karl Kuntz will not speak my name. He looks past me as I go. For the benefit of his sergeant should he be listening from the wardroom door, I say whatever nonsense a beggar would. I wheedle and wheeze. I shake the purse and laugh.

"Two thalers love the company of a third," I sing.

"Best see to your father," says Karl Kuntz, "It will not be long." The grave note in his voice straightens my stride.

"He has come," says my father in surprise. We are in the warm old rooms, now grown smaller and less bright. He means only me, that I have come. My father hooks his fingers into the marks on my cheeks, then presses his thumb into the mark on my brow.

"The world has already written you with its word," he says sadly. He lies back. He will not rise again.

"That's it?" I say, "Are we to finish so estranged?"

"Son," he says, "Go somewhere foreign. Find your war. Learn to love the road. Vagabond some. Here, we all know your nature too well. Your stories are too young for you to make legends of. I have said everything I know to say. Avoid future reunions of the family."

I look out at his drawer's bench leaned up against the wall. I think about the time he spent there. "But father," I say finally, "How will I answer if spoken to in foreign?"

"You must scamp understanding," says my father, "Devote yourself to dumb show. Shake your head like an insistent beast and make your word noises. Adopt the beggar's gait of your friend Pony. Let yourself be seen as simple."

"But I am not simple."

"If your foreigner is stubborn," says my father, "If he takes the imperative with you or points his finger at God, make your word noises per usual and then direct the inquisitor toward another unfortunate nearby. He will surely recognize the ruse. Shifting blame to others is how villains know their own."

So, Pony finally settles on a pony, a strong and stocky dun. And we make our move while the beast stands in harness after the schlepper departs to greet companions. When they send him back to his turnip cart to retrieve the desired wine, Pony is already in the cart, saying "Hop on Kuntz. We must away now with the whole package." There can be no dissembling or blame shifting, so we did away. We rattle over the stone bridge, with no thought given to the ban or pursuit.

The schlepper's stumpy legs give out soon after we depart the cobblestones. "You may cease flinging turnips, Kuntz," says Pony. And so I do. I lie back. We are on the high road now, absorbing the looks of many refugees, who must think we have adopted a dangerous direction.

"I apologize, Kuntz," says Pony. "I see in you neither guile nor hesitation. There is no horizon we might not cross into together." Although it is every man's duty to arrest thieves like us, no worthy peasant makes a play for the reins. Many familiar faces remark us and turn away. We have our new wine, a horse, and we're to go through the wood, headed for the Holy Land. We haven't a thought as to how this looks when viewed from above. At least I don't.

"How this little beast pleases me," says Pony some time later. "Like you, Kuntz, he only pulls harder when I stand the brake. Observe his heroic haunches as we climb to safety among these oaks." Pony then takes us up a narrow woodsman's track. The sudden change of grade suggests I sit up.

There I am, trying to maintain my place in a shifting bed of turnips. I am recalling when I first laid eyes on Pony, seated on his pony. It was a roan palfrey with an ornate blanket. It wore a tooled saddle with fine basket stirrups. I was, even then, the looky-loo to his lord. A sight like Pony mounted, seen today in the market square, would bring the sergeants with hooks on poles. Me, I saw him lose everything, just like I saw him lose the crowns. The saddle first. The blanket followed. The bridle, the spurs, the dashing hat of a cavalier. Pony hung to the roan palfrey until the final throw. "You, lad, are all that remains," he said that day.

As we top the rise, a great rearrangement shivers through the turnip bed. I totter, reaching, but tumble anyway. I forget how I came to be in the bramble. Nothing hurts yet but a wave is building. The last I see of Pony is him standing on the brake, hearing the cart come forward into the dun's legs causing a scramble, and then everything skids down the steep defile. A torrent of liberated vegetables scamper off into the undergrowth like a colony of plump white hares. I hear Pony trying to whoa a beast who doesn't yet recognize his voice. In the time I am turning away from thorns, the expected crash doesn't come. Ah, Pony, why did you not just rein in, unhitch your newly-acquired destrier? You might have gone to glory.

"Eltévedtünk, paraszt," says the Turk standing over me. "Hol van a folyó?"

"Search me," I shrug. So the Turk growls it again. His words sound like gravel sliding from a ledge. I get up and do a little dance. He does not touch his scimitar, so I point downhill. I copy his noises as best I can. The Turk sucks his teeth and smiles knowingly, begins sidling down the track, joining the conclave around the cart. The other Turks are laughing, holding the bridle and Pony at the shoulders. They're turning him around before the hangman and his sergeants. And there stands the jester. The Turks push Pony over. The jester looks long up into the trees, until he fixes the blind brass disks upon me.

"I am to prepare you for your confession," says the hangman. The first thing he says after putting an iron through my armpit. Now he turns the pincers in the coals. I am distracted. The jester, whose visor now features a wrought mustache and two clownish rings of teeth set into the metal, draws the bellows. I must be bleeding. "I will tell you when to speak," says the hangman, "And when to stop. Hold your peace for the moment." A part of me cannot make out what I am saying over my own distress. But what runs out of me is "Ask me."

Again and again.

"When you next speak," says the recording Lion, bent over his escritoire, the quill set into a sort of hook in place of his hand, "You will say your crime is proximity to the crime."

It goes the same with Pony. I am no longer bleeding. The jester is holding a compress to me. I was expecting a blade. I am again deafened by distress, but not my own. It is not my piece to confess, but I join my voice anyway. I keen it up from my very foundation. It was then that something heavy and unbidden slid into my mouth. I kneaded at the mysterious new plate with my tongue until I spit the crown into the jester's palm.

"Transport me abroad," I say with no permission, "Mark me to my rank or bend me to my oar. But do spend this for my brother's favor. Let his head find the basket in a stroke. Dissolve our sovereign bond."

The jester and the Lion put their heads together. First, they employ a wet knife. But the piece divides and then flows back into a golden whole. Nor can the tongs effect any lasting division. After a long moment, the Lion lowers his head.

"Will you hold it for us?" he asks the jester.

By what sorcery Pony transfers himself to me I know not. Perhaps it was the natural action of the irons which bit more than burned, seizing on meats within such that the Lion draws dark pieces into the light. My blood sizzles away and is commingled with that of Pony, thereby annealed on the same iron. We are drawn, Pony and I, through the same glowing eye of the nips. I think I was first. Or it is the other way around? In any case, we are diminished by the same simple machine; I cannot now say in what order. I see Pony standing at the rock. I see myself standing in the crowd, held up by no cousin, doing the best I can. I see Pony kneel but feel the cold gneiss on my kneecaps. He makes his final appeal to the public, to all the cousins in turn— to everyone not holding me up: "Kuntz

Stainal the farm hand, Kuntz Rhünagel the laborer, Kuntz Pütner the farm hand." Nobody
answers or stirs. "Every man a murderer!" cries
Pony. He twists his bleeding neck to address
the headsman, hefting his brutal tool. Pony's
voice becomes constrained by his uncomfort-
able posture. "The only witnesses were Turks,"
lies Pony. "You've got the wrong Kuntz."

And then he, we, are forever divided.

TO SEE A BLACK DEVIL

John Daker

I have a cousin who is a ranger for the National Park Service out west and he has seen things that would chill your blood. Missing people found dead in impossible places, stairs built in the woods where no building ever stood, and trees with a dozen freshly-severed human hands nailed to it. He's also seen Bigfoot. The city is not immune to this kind of strangeness, either. Not even Dallas.

Cities are strange places. I was doing a stakeout once, looking for evidence of a philandering husband. I know, I know, stereotypical P.I. stuff, but it pays the bills—sometimes. I was out in front of this diner. Sally's. Don't bother looking it up. There is no documentation, beyond my account, that it exists. After sitting outside in my '98 Hyundai Sonata with its malfunctioning air conditioner for two hours, I noticed that no one went in or out. I had to leak the lizard, so I aimed my smartphone at the location I was watching and went inside. Everyone ignored me. Everyone. Did a quick head count and the place was exactly half full. A perfect diversity rainbow of people. I swear, every possible combination of race and sex was in there. Went into the men's room, did my business, and came out. Every single person in the diner was different. Even the staff. Still diverse, but the faces were not the same. Every seat that had been full was empty and every seat that had been empty was now full.

I got out of there was fast as politely possible and returned to my Hyundai. The phone had been recording the whole time. The place I was watching was next door to Sally's, but you could still see the front door of the diner. Later, when I looked, it hadn't captured me going in and out. But that's not why you came to talk to me. You want to know what happened to the body of Hans Meller.

"There are two things not written down officially, but you might want to know. First, Meller's last words before his execution were 'For dealing with me this way, you will have to see a black devil!' The second thing, his last request, was to wear a particular pair of red knitted wool stockings. The request was denied," said the female police officer. She was no lady. Her hair was not even shoulder length. I suspected she took testosterone to bulk up. She had a sort of in-between body shape, something between a woman and a man, not committing to one or the other. "I got the file here, Mister Schmidt," she said.

"One moment, Officer Suarez, I have not agreed to take this case," I said.

"Let me tell you a little story, Mister Private Dick," she continued, emphasizing that last word in an entirely antagonistic way. "A certain stacked brunette at the Department of Public Safety happens to have a license renewal for a dick. She just so happens to have a cousin who is a police officer needing jobs done from time to time. If the police officer tells her cousin—who has never had to buy her own drink at a bar—that she is disappointed with her dick, his license renewal might get denied. But it's just a story."

"You've got me by the balls," I said. I agreed to the pittance she was offering and left the police station. My credit score was dropping faster than my ex's panties when Roscoe bought her a drink, so I had to earn some cash any way I could. Not only was I behind on the rent, but the alimony as well. Since it all went up Roscoe's nose, she was always squawking if it was even a day late. This Meller case would hold off the collection agencies for a little while. You've seen the case files; you know what his crimes were. You know that his body went missing after a freak power outage. The body was what they wanted. Now it was my responsibility to track it down.

The useless talking heads in the media had not yet been told about the empty execution chamber, so I did not have to deal with a media circus every time I went to interview someone. I started with the people who were present at the execution. In addition to the slack-jawed prison guards too inept to be cops and the warden, I spoke to the grieving sister of the most recent victim. Now, despite what the warden said later, I did not ask her out on a date. She was as hot as the fires of hell where Hans is hopefully burning and I struggled not to stare at her chest as she spoke. Nothing anyone said was different than what is in the file. I had hoped to glean some new information out of them, but there was nothing. The power had flickered only for one second, not enough time to get the body out before the cameras recovered, even if everybody was in on it. I didn't like the idea of a supernatural bodysnatcher, but that was the closest thing to a theory anyone had. And I don't know what you believe or don't believe, but we can all agree that supernatural body snatchers aren't real. Well, I used to be able to agree to that.

My investigation was not going anywhere until the judge that sentenced Meller died. He had been found strangled with a red knitted wool stocking. That was the detail the police did not release. The red stocking was my guide. He had been found on the roof of his house. The windows were all shut. There was a thin layer of dust over everything. The place had not been disturbed in a while. There was no ladder anywhere nearby. Nor any evidence that anyone had been on the roof at all. A giant bird just picked him up and gently placed him on the shingles.

The stocking was consistent with those Hans wished to wear during his execution. All the door jambs in the house were damaged as if Goliath was hunting down David for revenge. I spoke with the cop who wore sunglasses in the house in order to hide his perpetual hangover and learned that only one stocking had been used in the crime. Where was the second one? Stuck to the wall of the dryer? Surely the killer wasn't wearing them. Winter in Texas rarely justifies wool socks.

I needed a lead. So, I took a trip to Oak Lawn to meet with Gary the Glutton. He collected worker's comp from some sort of injury that stopped him from working, but it did not stop him from spending all his time eating at local restaurants. Despite the name, he was quite thin, which he said was due to a glandular disorder. I did not doubt that, but I doubted that he was permanently unable to work. No insurance company ever paid me to investigate, so I didn't look into it. He knew the comings and goings of all sorts of people. I found him a good resource for information and his price was merely a meal. This time, he wanted to go to a hole-in-the-wall Mexican place where good mariachi music was ruined by being played through cheap speakers.

"So, you're looking for the missing body of Hans Meller?" Gary asked between bites of a taco or enchilada or burrito. All Mexican food is just a tortilla with meat, cheese, and maybe beans. Who can tell the difference?

"That hasn't been reported to the press," I said, watching melted cheese dribble down his chin. "How did you know that?"

"I was banging this broad and she told me that her cop cousin was tasked into looking into it. People talk, especially when they think no one is listening . She said they got some dumbass private investigator involved, so I immediately thought of you," he said.

"No offense taken," I said. I was quite offended. I didn't want to feed Gary any more than I had to. I needed his information more than my ego needed reinforcement. I waited while another chipful of cheesy bean slop disappeared into his maw before he spoke again.

"Don't look into this Meller matter anymore. Walk away. No good will come of it," he said. I should have listened. But I needed to eat, too. So I had to pursue it further. And I certainly wasn't going to spend who knows how much on this meal without some good information.

"Listen, Gary, my license is on the line. And I don't leave anything undone. This meal is on me," I said, "Surely you've got something."

Gary's eyes widened as a couple of beans fell from his gaping maw. "Fine. May the consequences of this fall on your head, not mine." Gary whispered while holding a chip dripping with red salsa. "You didn't hear this from me, but if you go to Fredericksburg, you will learn more." He finished his meal and I dug through my credit cards, trying to find one that I wasn't too far behind on. I asked the waitress if the receipt could show one Seis Hombres platter instead . Like all the women I have ever met, she didn't find what I said funny and ignored me.

That night, I returned to my rundown studio to plan my trip. As usual, I took the long way around back, so that I could avoid the dope slingers and their customers who always asked for money that clogged the main entrance. The payout from this case was too important and I needed to solve it quick. My creditors were no longer taking any more excuses; they wanted cold cash, not hot air. While packing, I called up the local Motel 6 to book a room.

"You're in luck. there is just one room left," said the clerk before quoting me a price that was half my monthly rent. I didn't mind, I figured I could submit an expense report to the police. Even if they didn't cough up, I was sure I could slip it by the Internal Revenue Service as a business expense. But I had a question for the clerk.

"I know you don't set the prices—and I will pay it, but why so high?"

"Supply and demand," the clerk said. "We're full up from all the Bigfoot hunters. They're all here to make a name for themselves."

I paid and hung up the phone. Then I pulled up the news for the Fredericksburg area and saw something that chilled my blood. Bigfoot sightings in the Fredericksburg area have increased 750 percent over the past few days, it read.

Next, I pulled up the dates of the sightings. The sightings increased the same day as Meller's execution. And it wasn't just an increase of one sighting a month instead of one sighting a year—no, this was multiple sightings every single night. The coincidence strolled through my mind like the subject of the Patterson-Gimlin film. There was a clear connection between the two events. I sat in my chair and wrote down the things I needed: my flashlight, extra ammunition for my revolver, and my aluminum-foil-lined fanny pack for kolaches. I was so preoccupied with the list that I did not hear the thing approach from behind. It wrapped a red stocking around my neck. It tightened and the scent of rotten eggs filled my nostrils.

"Chemosh has been called. Chemosh is coming for you, mortal," it said.

I clutched at the stocking and tried to pull it off so I could breathe. "Chemosh?" I said, thinking it was a pseudonym of one of the shady people I owed money to. "The check is in the mail." The thing responded by pulling harder. My hand swept across my desk as I tried to reach for my revolver, while the other pulled on the stocking just enough to let a little air through. In my flailing, the gun fell off of the desk and onto the floor. I thrust my elbow back into the thing. I felt animal fur against my skin, not human body hair or whatever else the cops wrote in their report.

I must have hit a sensitive spot because the thing screeched and dropped the stocking in my lap. I dove for my fallen gun. I turned to a black humanoid more than a head higher than me. It ducked through my front door. A black devil or a Bigfoot, take your pick. My lungs were working overtime to get oxygen to my body, but I forced myself to pursue Chemosh. With the hour being late, none of my neighbors were out in the hallway and it ran faster than I thought possible while making next to no noise. That must have been how it had snuck up on me so easily. A thought came to me as I tried to chase Chemosh by following the faint scent it left behind: How had it gotten in? I always locked the door to my apartment.

Through the halls and down four flights of stairs, I hurried after Chemosh, always just out of sight, so I could not get a clear picture of what it was. Once I reached the bottom of the stairs, I figured I would get a better view of it. As I stepped out of the complex, the streetlights lit up the thing. It was a Bigfoot or Sasquatch or Harry or whatever you want to call it. The Bigfoot lumbered across the street, ignoring the traffic, simply stepping around or past the cars that zipped by. No one honked or braked as it crossed through the streets. How could no one see a thing that large? It disappeared down an alley across the street. No way that I was going to play Frogger tonight to chase an American Bigfoot in Dallas.

I went back up to my apartment and called the police. The rotten egg smell had disappeared, but the red stocking was still there. The whole thing was not a dream.

The officer who came to take my statement was a slovenly man in an ill-fitting uniform. He approached me with a coffee-stained notebook and a pen. The cap of the pen looked like it spent more time being chewed than on the end of the pen. How the Dallas PD allowed him to represent the force of law and order was a mystery I was not being paid to solve, so I didn't think about it too much.

"Let's start from the beginning. What happened?" the officer asked.

"I was choked by a big hairy demonic man-thing! We struggled for a bit, I chased it out to the street, and it fled through the alley across the street with the overflowing dumpster."

"And then you came back to your apartment to find that the tooth fairy put a quarter under your pillow?" he asked. I quietly took a deep breath before handing him the red stocking as proof of my claims. The officer looked at it incredulously.

"This is your proof?"

"Yes," was all I could say. He left without any further words.

When the sun finally rose, I slept. I woke facing the door, revolver in hand. My dreams were of chasing the Bigfoot through the woods. The laughter of Hans Meller—a man I had never met—haunted my every step.

After a few hours of sleep, I got up, loaded my Sonata with the things I needed and started the drive to Fredericksburg. At the kolache shop half-way, I was charged for three kolaches but, once on the road again, found I only received two. Both went into the fanny pack for later. The town of Fredericksburg was hopping. At the Motel 6, I was surrounded by men in camouflage with enough freeze-dried food, guns, ammunition, knives, and water purifying tablets to survive any sort of apocalypse: nuclear, zombie, or Biblical. Snatches of stories of alleged encounters, prideful boasts of hunting prowess, and contradictory theories on the ecology of the Sasquatch floated through the motel lobby. One guy, who was wearing a green beret as if he were some special forces badass said he spent his time in the military hunting Bigfoots in Kentucky. If they knew the truth of what was out there, if they knew that Chemosh had killed at least one person, they would not be so cavalier about their chances to bag it.

"I'm a victim of economics," said the old man who checked me in. I think he was excusing himself for the sky-high rate. He looked me in the eye. "You've actually seen a Bigfoot, haven't you?" he asked after handing me my room key. This fellow knew more than he let on about the people he interacted with.

"I don't know what you are talking about," I replied, not wanting to admit to anything.

"Standing pat," he said. "Wise. There is something going on here, something dark. I don't know what it is or why you came, but nothing good will come of this Bigfoot madness. Other than what comes to my pocketbook."

I went to the room and dropped off my luggage. Although I was tired, I decided to at least get a bite to eat. I found a little German place on Main Street and had a pleasant dish of schnitzel and spätzle washed down with a fine lager. The chaos of the full restaurant felt normal, something I had not felt since the beginning of the Hans Meller matter. A few seats here and there were empty, but there was no discernable pattern. The sightings were what was on everyone's lips. As I ate, I listened and learned that there had been a cluster of recent sightings southwest of town.

After driving back to the motel with a full stomach, I fell asleep with my revolver next to the bed. Dreams of being stalked through the streets of Dallas late at night kept my sleep from being restful. That morning, I took my camping gear and drove south for about twenty minutes until a feeling of dread came over me like a noose tightening around my neck.

Berry bushes were starting to appear on either side of the road. I knew this was the place where I would find answers or annihilation.

I pulled over and got out. I had a compass and my fully-charged phone's GPS to help guide me back. I wasn't too worried about getting lost. That was the arrogant city boy in me speaking, the one I wish I didn't listen to. The feeling of dread pulled me deeper into the woods. Normally, dread makes a man fight or flee, but this was like a magnet to my soul. I couldn't resist it. Every few minutes, I patted the revolver on my hip.

It started to get dark, so I set up camp for the night in a clearing. There was a tall tree that seemed to have frightened off most of the rest of the plant life, but not the birds. They sat together in pairs on the surrounding trees, like awkward married couples wearing matching shirts in public. I had read enough information online on how to set up a campfire, so after twenty minutes of work, I had a little fire going. I fished a kolache out of my fanny pack and ate it as I planned the best spot to put the tent. After I got my tent set up, I waited, gun in hand. For Chemosh.

I felt a drop of liquid land on my forehead and dribble down my face. I wiped it off and, by the light of the fire, I saw that it was blood. I looked into upper branches of the tree overhead and the man in the green beret from the motel was looking down on me. His head was twisted around. Blood dripped from his open mouth. It didn't take a coroner to know that he was dead. There were no branches that I could reach, even if I jumped. How had he climbed up there? There was no ladder nearby or marks on the trunk from any spiked shoes or climbing equipment.

Something told me I shouldn't dwell on the ruined man in the tree. I turned in time to see the Sasquatch approach. I think Chemosh hoped I would be so distracted by the corpse that I would be easy prey. My hand went to the revolver and I fired a shot directly into its leg. Chemosh roared with a sound that I can only describe as a chimpanzee burning in Hell.

I ran past it, scooped my pack off the ground, left my tent, and ran in the direction of my car. Thank goodness I had left a GPS marker where I parked. Even still, going through the woods at night is a terrible idea. I could hear Chemosh behind me and every time I thought I lost it, I would hear that ear-splitting screech a little too close for comfort. I don't know how I stayed ahead of it, but I did. Branches scratched my face and I knew I left a blood trail it could track.

I have never been so relieved to see my crummy, air condionter-less, dented-from-the-shopping-carts-of-irresponsible-people Hyundai. Unlike every horror movie I had ever watched, all my technology worked perfectly: the cell phone, the flashlight, and the car. The car surprised me the most. That old jalopy had a habit of breaking down at the worst possible time, such as when merging onto I-635. In the light of my flashlight, I saw a scrap of paper under the windshield wiper.

A few times, I thought I saw a dark humanoid shape lurking just outside of what my headlights illuminated, but nothing happened on the ride back to the motel. I waited until I was back at the motel to read the paper. A receipt for Sally's, dated for that day. I stayed up past midnight watching the door and window, waiting for Chemosh. In the twilight zone between night and morning, I looked at the receipt again.

The date had changed to the new day. The address, too, had changed. Still in Dallas, but it was a few streets over from the location I had the misfortune of entering in the past. Speaking of misfortune, it was next door to where I met that cheating whore. This was no coincidence, someone—or more accurately—something was deliberately messing with me. The next stage of my investigation was clear, but I was not sure I wanted answers. My pride, my private investigator's license, and my bank account said otherwise.

After a late morning coffee, I headed to the front desk. The clerk looked over the numerous scratches on my face as he processed my checkout paperwork.

"Pissed off a housecat?" the clerk asked.

"No, I took a walk in the woods and fell down."

"Did you see Dave out there? His buddies have been looking for him. He was the chubby one in the beret."

I said I hadn't seen him and finished checking out. I put it at a 50/50 chance that Dave's body would ever be found. I didn't know which would be worse: the body being found or it being lost forever.

I got in my car and went straight to the address on the receipt. I was tired, but I had to see the end of this matter. Stopped several times on the trip for more coffee and to deal with the natural consequences of drinking, by my estimation, a gallon of coffee over the entire day. You can't call yourself a coffee drinker until you have survived a whole day of subpar black coffee from cheap motels and gas stations.

I pulled up to Sally's. I openly wore my revolver, knowing it probably wouldn't help, but it certainly made me feel better. I took a deep breath and walked inside. Inside it was 1956. Any movie director would do what actresses normally did for their parts in order to get such a perfect set for his mid-century period piece. One seat open, a small table with a single chair in the center of the dining room.

Lady Bird Johnson was my waitress. She put a menu down in front of me, and just sauntered away. No words were exchanged. The whole place was quiet other than the sounds of cutlery scraping across plates and chewing. The menu—a freshly laminated thing that I instinctively knew I was the first customer to ever touch—only had one meal listed on it. A hansburger and freyes. I re-read it several times to make sure I read it correctly. Yes, that was exactly what was written upon it.

As soon as I made that revelation, the waitress returned with a plate containing a hamburger, fries, and two hush puppies. I thanked Ladybird. She said nothing and sauntered through the kitchen door. I poked at the food with my fork and while the fries seemed normal, the hush puppies and the hamburger were wrong. I'm not a spiritual person normally, but I think God was looking out for me in that moment.

During my probing, the fried skin of the hush puppies split open to reveal an eyeball staring back at me. No one reacted to my little outburst, or my tumbled chair. I drew my gun and took a step toward the kitchen. I heard a couple dozen forks hitting a plate in perfect synchronization and every diner at Sally's turned their soulless eyes to me. I made my way to the kitchen. I still feel them watching me.

I opened the door and saw two human bodies laid out on tables. One was Hans Meller and the other was the judge. I looked at Hans a little closer and his eyes were missing, as was a hamburger patty-sized chunk from his left arm.

The waitress appeared in front of me. I knew she could not actually be Lady Bird Johnson, but she looked just like her. When she spoke, she even sounded like her.

"Say my name," she purred. "You have been pursuing me and I want you to know that you have my full attention."

"I don't know your name," I replied.

"But I have told you my name. Just say it and I will give you the body of Hans Meller. You will get your payday. But in so doing, know that you are allowing me free reign in this world. Just say my name."

I don't go to little diners anymore. I am on a first-name basis with every maître-d' in all the best restaurants in Highland Park. I do not reserve. If I show up, I get a table. Not just any table, mind you—a good one. My table never fails to impress my date.

Until my arrival, there were no residences at Reunion Tower. Officially, there still aren't.

My penthouse is where the restaurants used to be. When I leave my home, I escort the aspiring model, wanna-be singer, or whoever I am with that week down to the ground floor in my private elevator. My Tesla never needs charging. Nor do I need to worry about routine maintenance; I know that the car will always function perfectly. Except the radio. It only plays Christmas music, except at Christmas time. Christmas, it only plays the screams of the damned.

THE KOBOLD'S STARE

Jeffro Johnson

It's all over thirty feet into the dungeon.

The newly-minted, first-level fighter falls into a pit. Green players, unfamiliar with how quickly little problems spiral out of control, are the only ones able to brush off the sense of foreboding. Why worry so early? After all, the fighter is only injured. Fishing him out of the pit will be straightforward. It is self-evident that his tumble will be nothing more than a minor speed bump on the straight road to gold and fame. The players are discussing how best to use their ten-foot poles, iron spikes, and fifty-foot lengths of rope when the dungeon master asks them to roll for initiative.

Here come kobolds emerging from the shadows nearby! Only six of them. No big deal. The players abandon their associate in the pit for the moment to attend to this new threat. The diminutive, dog-headed monsters throw their spears. The party's cleric is injured by a lucky hit. The players respond at close quarters with melee weapons, killing two of the dog men.

In spite of the danger, it is inconceivable to the players that they might have to cancel the delve at this point. The players elect to fight on, thinking that the tide should turn in their favor—especially if initiative goes their way. The next round, the players are informed that ominous skittering sounds are coming from the west. The players drop another kobold, but lose their dwarf to the melee. A disaster! The fighter is in the pit trap, the cleric is hurt, the magic-user is out of spells, the dwarf is out of play. This party is pretty well exhausted.

At this point, the dungeon master explains that giant rats have arrived. Several have leaped into the pit and begun tearing apart the abandoned fighter. Thoughts of expeditious retreat now turn to outright panic as the fighter's screams echo off the cavern walls. When the players turn to leave, they discover the entrance is now blocked by eight more kobolds that have just come down from the trees.

This is the end.

Unless somebody has a particularly brilliant idea right now, every single character in the party is set to be killed, captured, or served up as a main course to a host of dog men. Even if the party manages to get out of this, they are still down at least two player characters and have less than nothing to show for their first adventure. Incredibly, the players will have spent more time rolling up their characters than they did actually playing.

What is this game that manages to transport its players to a world of brutality and horror?

Well, the box it came in was purple. Its rule book was red with a surreal green dragon on the cover. The game module? *The Keep on the Borderlands*. Elder hobbyists would look askance at this release, dismissing it as "kiddie D&D." Played as written, however, the module was a particularly grisly package. For millions of kids entering the world of *Dungeons & Dragons* for the very first time in 1981, this outcome was as familiar as it was inevitable.

Not too many years before, the owner of a brand new role-playing game faced mapping out a half-dozen levels of an original underworld environment. Referees of *Tunnels & Trolls* were tasked with "digging" a dungeon with only the barest hints. The *Metamorphosis Alpha* purchaser similarly accepted the burden of mapping out seventeen starship decks, each twenty-five miles across. What kind of challenges were to be placed in these environments? How severe should they be? Everything was entirely up to the referee.

The young kids that couldn't imagine creating that kind of original material in bulk? If they grasped any of the rules and trusted Gygax to set things up for them with the game module, then the purchaser of the second *Basic D&D* set was being given a Rube

Goldberg-style death machine that would easily wipe out his players' characters within one to three sessions.

Granted, *Basic D&D* wasn't the only game at the time that was sure to crush the young gamer's dreams of making it big, striking it rich, and then retiring a beloved character to a castle not too terribly remote from civilization. The typical autoduelist in *Car Wars* would die an uninspiring death in his first amateur night event. Even a successful professional duelist was sure to end up in a high-speed collision that would see both the car and the character going up in flames after three or four arena events. *Melee* and *Wizard* characters entering into their respective arenas as well faced the harsh reality of a winning streak that went no farther than three or four matches.

Losing even one of them meant death.

Fantasy roleplaying games are different, though. Somehow people expect to play the same character for months on end just by default. They want to buy a miniature that they paint up in order to perfectly represent THEIR GUY. They want to hire someone to create a portrait of their favorite character, something they will treasure always. Today it's not uncommon for people to work up overwrought backstories of their characters that can run for several pages. Even the time it takes to put a character together has exploded from a few minutes to a few hours—or even a few days!

But just imagine it. All of your best friends have come over and you are going to play this exciting new game. Everyone rolls up their characters and in a matter of hours, the players find themselves in a cave with an army of giant rats on one side and a group of kobolds blocking the exit. One player character is already dead on the ground. Another, trapped at the bottom of a pit, is being torn apart by the rats. There doesn't seem to be anything on the character sheet that can stop what is happening.

Can you as a referee go on making call after call, impartially adjudicating the rules that will more than likely see each and every player character die within the next ten minutes? Can you as a player accept this outcome as it transpires? Will you find something to argue about? Or flip the table? Or stomp off in a huff, declaring that you will never play again? Not everyone has the courage or the grace to allow the game to run its course. But that is precisely the sort of thing this strange old game expected everyone to do.

A great deal hinges on how your group deals with the matter.

Those who recoil at the idea of killing even one player character will tend to play a story-oriented game where the rules are largely ignored and the dice are routinely fudged on the dungeon master's part in order to create the sort of outcomes he requires for his overarching plots. Even those that have a modest amount of self-respect will be tempted to make all manner of changes to the game. Some will grow lenient with regards to what constitutes a "hopeless character" or else devise elaborate attribute rollings mechanics that ensure the player characters are properly heroic. Others will start characters at maximum hit points at first level or will allow players to skip the first few character levels entirely. Still others will dole out "hero points" that will allow the players to ignore hits that could potentially lay them low or else allow them to alter the outcome of any dice result not to their liking.

The sheer range of house rules and variant systems that have been devised to address this really goes to show just how far people will go to avoid having these glorified chess pawns meet an untimely demise. But people who play that way are not at all the same types of people as the generation that first received the game.

That death was understood to be a touchstone of *D&D* is evident from the 1985 treatment of the game by *Sixty Minutes*. The TV news show described several teens whose deaths were linked to the game thusly: "Timothy Grice, 21. Shotgun suicide. The detective report noted *D&D* became a reality. Irving 'Bink' Pulling, 16, an avid *D&D* player. A suicide. Daniel and Steven Erwin. 16 and 12. A murder and a suicide. The police said they were obsessed with the game. James Alan Kearbey, 14 years old. Charged with killing his junior high school principal and wounding three other people. Police are blaming D&D."

This gruesome, real-life body count purportedly spawned by the game is striking, no doubt, even if such cases were insignificant next to a player base that was easily three million strong. Of course, if you thought otherwise, a letter from TSR's legal department could go a long way toward helping you see things differently. Nevertheless, urban legends surrounding the game would persist for decades. Fear of occult societies operating under the veneer of everyday American life only added to the mystique of the game.

For the typical small town evangelical with little more than a stray Chick tract to go on, *D&D* was serious business. One day you're playing what you think is just a bewildering game run by a mysterious and attractive dungeon mistress. Later you find out that the game procedures were actually occult rituals, preparing you for induction into a real life witches coven where you would soon master the arts of casting real life magic spells. Washing out of a campaign by losing your thief to a failed saving throw against the poisoned dart that you missed on that last treasure chest? This is something that is so devestating, so tremendous that you would be liable to kill yourself over it.

For one brief shining moment *D&D* was more than some kind of lame pastime for slovenly nerds. It was dangerous. It was a game that was so immersive it would cause you to lose your capacity to differentiate between fantasy and reality. In the placid world of a suburban America where kids could still play outside unattended until the street lights came on, *D&D* was a threat ten times more sinister than heavy metal or drugs or even lp records that produced secret messages when played backwards.

D&D was cool. But the suspicion and hostility directed at the game derived not just from the purported spiritual threat it posed. Even in its heyday of mass market success it was somehow a relic from another era, completely out of step with the times.

The people that put *D&D* together really were fundamentally different from us. Its creators came of age watching spaghetti westerns where the line between heroes and villains is blurred in a remote frontier where gritty violence is the order of the day. Science fiction epics featured kitschy post-apocalyptic bunker settings where anyone reaching the age of thirty was put to death, or showed life on board fantastic spaceships where crazed botanists killed their crewmates and reprogrammed all the robots in order to preserve the last trees in existence, or where a lone policeman living hand to mouth in an overpopulated city gradually came to the the grim realization the popular processed food product that everyone depended on for survival had gone from being made out of seaweed to being made out of people.

Movies like *First Blood* didn't even exist in the seventies. Even a truly inspirational film like *Rocky* which signaled what was about to become a tremendous change of tides within the culture, were pretty low key. Rocky didn't need to be the greatest boxer in the world. Heck, he didn't even need to win the match. He was just some nobody punching sides of beef in a meat packing plant whose only desire was to "go the distance" by lasting fifteen rounds in the ring with Apollo Creed.

1978's *The Deer Hunter* was a similarly restrained. It showed just how devastating the Vietnam War could be to a tight-knit group of friends from a small Pennsylvanian town. The three guys didn't last even one battle before they were captured, put inside horrific cages, submerged in a dirty river, and then forced to play Russian Roulette. Their escape is neither exciting nor uplifting. One of them is forced to have his legs amputated. He is so humiliated by this he remains at the VA hospital for as long as he can manage rather than return home to face day-to-day life as only half a man. Another of them is so lost to madness he cannot even know to flee Saigon as the war enters its final stage.

The fantasy adventure game of the the first waves of *D&D Basic Sets* were of a piece with the kind of human fragility on display in *The Deer Hunter*. The too-perfect fantasy worlds of Jeff Easly featuring impeccably dressed girl band types standing around looking dramatic were not even imaginable in this antediluvian world. But it wouldn't last.

Just a few short years later, a ninety-pound woman would duct tape a plasma rifle to a flamethrower and blithely enter the lair of an alien queen all by herself. The most terrifying unstoppable robot monster out of all of future history got demoted to some kid's sidekick. An off-duty policemen celebrated Christmas by clearing every floor of Nakatomi Towers of elite German terrorists. And countless muscle-bound action heroes routinely found a way to outdo entire countries worth of armed forces.

A series of blockbuster films rewired the minds of an entire generation to the point where they could no longer conceive playing the game that Gary Gygax had helped develop. With Gary Gygax forced out of his position as CEO of TSR, Inc, the game could begin its gradual transformation into a fundamentally different type of game altogether.

Granted, a whole lot of things were called D&D that weren't really D&D even at the time. There were the TSR *Endless Quest* books by Rose Estes—*Choose Your Own Adventure* knockoffs with D&D branding and titles like *Return to Brookmere* and *Pillars of Pentegarn*. There was the moderately sanitized version of the game sold in Toys "R" Us and Kay Bee Toys in the form of the Frank Mentzer *Basic/Expert/ Companion/Master/Immortal* sets. There was the Saturday morning cartoon series that presented a freaky sort of funhouse version of the game. Later on there would even be fairly sophisticated computer game adaptations in the form of SSI's *Gold Box* series which began with *The Pool of Radiance*.

The 1980s was witness to a deluge of D&D -themed merchandise, but somehow the concept of the game retained its identity in spite of it. No one picking up the alternate media adaptations of the property was confused. Indeed, most people purchasing them were all too aware of the fact that they didn't have a first-rate gaming group that could actually play the real thing.

As decades passed the spirit of the game weathered threats on manifold fronts: a lackluster second edition that removed the teeth from the game, a descent into grid gaming fueled by tacky game design techniques pioneered with *Magic* cards and computer games like *Diablo*, tedious Nerdsploitation television in the form of *The Big Bang Theory*. As bad as these developments were, D&D at least remained a moderately esoteric game that you would play with your friends.

All of that changed when a group of voice actors figured out that they could score a pretty good gig by posting their D&D sessions on YouTube. Never before could so many wrong ideas about gaming be communicated so persuasively to so many. Boomers might have birthed the hobby, pushing lead on sprawling sand tables in their basements. Gen X might have taken it up in countless all night game sessions during endless summertime sleepovers. Today, people can skip these years of actual gaming and instead learn everything they need to know just by watching theater kids try to out-cringe each other on YouTube.

The extent to which the game has fallen can be summed up by a single Tweet from Matt Mercer:

If you need to take some time to process, that is ok. Just know there is trust and agreement at our table for this game and the challenges it offers. The darkest moments often lead to the brightest epiphanies. Love you all.

It's bizarre, really.

When a player character dies in one of these "actual play" shows and their spectators are spoken to as if they are being consoled after the shock of losing a close relative. The players are spoken of as if they have made an explicit concession to each other to occasionally entertain some kind of setback in the course of play. And the game itself? The game is transformed from an amusing pastime, to something more akin to a religious experience.

This is a long, long way from a healthy twelve-year-old dutifully stocking the Caverns of Quasqueton from the monster and treasure lists in the back of *In Search of the Unknown*. And thanks to the popularity of the show, there is no shortage of people eager to explain how much D&D has "evolved" and why no one who likes what it used to be has a right to complain about the changes.

What's it like? To save you from the experience of watching it, I'll break it down for you:

The locations where gameplay takes place are introduced with extensive, rambling monologues loaded down with countless made-up fantasy names and florid descriptions.

As new player characters enter the game, special care is taken by the player to describe their clothing and jewelry. Each one must have an original funny voice for engaging in improvised dialogue with the other characters.

The dungeon master will have figures and a high-quality diorama prepared for each session's combat, which will last anywhere from thirty minutes to two hours out of a four-hour session.

The players will prepare to be hyperenthusiastic about engaging with whatever scene or situation the dungeon master has prepared for them, but they will not expect to make any significant strategic decisions.

The players will become particularly active when their personal initiative turn comes up during the battles, but they will rarely put their heads together to come up with an elaborate plan.

Whenever they deal a sufficient amount of damage to a foe in battle, the DM will turn to them with a wry grin and ask, "How do you want to do this?" At this point the narrative is temporarily ceded to the player so that he can describe some weird cartoon-like finishing move that sounds like something out of Mortal Kombat. Similarly, if the player character is knocked down or killed during battle, he will be given the spotlight for a moment to describe the wistful thoughts he might have about his lame backstory as he fades in and out of consciousness.

And when it really is a full-on player character death that has developed in the course of play? The entire table will slump in their chairs with hang-dog looks that will last for hours. Afterwards, the DM will have to draft a perfectly-worded announcement to prepare viewers for what will no doubt be a devastating blow, on likely to require careful management of all five stages of grief. This is not the voice of a dungeon master commenting on the surprising results of a Thursday night game session that took an unexpected turn. It comes off more like any of the dozen memorandums you're likely to get from your HR department each week.

This new conception of the game is abominable merely because it has ceased to be a game. It's a disaster because it is so completely inverted it has ceased to be an escape.

No matter. There are, after all, much more pressing matters to attend to. Back at a gaming table that no one will ever bother to record video of or broadcast on YouTube, the players have just finished rolling up their replacement characters. After much discussion, they have a number of ideas about how to handle the caves and are eager to see what the dice have to say about them.

This time they might just be able to take those kobolds!

DEATH IN PETZU MAAL

C.D. Crabtree

I.

It was the monsoon season when he came, the season of water and muddy earth, the season when red mud buries villages and dynasties, the season when blood washes away quickly saving the women much scrubbing. It was the monsoon season and I do not think he expected that.

His west is dry. Yellow spiked plants drink up all the moisture leaving only dust on the ground, in the air, on precious skin. I know this because I journeyed there once on a state visit where my father wished to present his young daughter to the House of Andoh as a candidate for a marriage match.

When he came into Petzu Maal on that desert slinker, slimmer and faster than the slinker of the mountains, more treacherous than the slinker of the jungle, the qualmos laughed at him as only peasants can laugh. They pointed and their jaws hung open. They rocked their gourd-shaped heads back and forth, spilling water from the woven leaves they use as hats. He rode past them barebacked on that evil lizard and they leaped away from its wickedly barbed tail. Let the mudfooted peasants laugh. He didn't even look at them.

The day was bright and A'a shone above him through a mist of rainwater fractured into all the colors of corn. The barbarian rode his sinuous slinker through that curtain of water and into my world.

Bronzed as the rocks in the parched lands of his birth but lighter than the olive-skinned wetland warriors of Petzu Maal, a blood of living fire ran in his veins.

I was in the Blue Court of Lilypond in the company of the Noble Tsherl of Clan Szim when he entered my vetch. I was Tsherl's acknowledged consort but I followed the stranger with my eyes. After all, the Lilypond was mine. The Blue Court, Red Court, Court of Love, and Court of Revelry, painted by the best artisans in the city, all surrounded my pond with its lilypads and sacred frogs. The priests of A'a and of Xitil Xavo Kan the Axe of Justice blessed these walls, baked tile roofs, and my pond, twice a year. I paid them well to do it.

Lilypond vetch was where the best came to drink, to revel, to live.

Tsherl was as cold as the western barbarian was hot. He was a stone under a mountain waterfall, but quick and deadly as a swamp adder. His weapon was the stingray spine, forearm shield, and the short copper axe. I had seen him use them many times. His movements were beautiful, like the play of rippling waters or the notes of the kun-pipe at dawn when a jaguar retreats from the clearing and all that is seen are the eyes, dancing. These were his weapons. And his cutting tongue. And his pride. And his poetry. His lovemaking, too. The last cuts deeper than any axe.

In contrast to the cold hardness of the Jaguar Noble Tsherl, the barbarian stranger had hot eyes and hot skin. His lovemaking was an embrace of molten earth. He was a rock jutting from the desert, an outcrop of the Parched Hills, staring unblinking into the sandstorm of life. His hands branded my soul. Strong fingers and a shaggy ginger mane were tongues of the fire upon my skin. How could I not love him?

He bore green death in burning hands, a sword—as the westerners often use, ironwood hilted, the blade a shining single green stone I couldn't place. A tapering serpent sharp and cruel, it lay on the stone table before his dripping, heavy, form. That sword was green death in a city turned green by moss and lichen and the green hearts of envy in every citizen. Which death was greener, that of ancient Petzu Maal or the mysterious sword of the west?

I signaled Squash to bring him a drink. Not sour beer but t'chal, the liquid fire of the west. "Break the seal on a jar of that shipment of t'chal the monks of Blood Valley brought us last season."

The Noble Tsherl watched me as I walked past my qualmo servant. I excused myself.

Squash did not show surprise. I doubt he could have even registered it. Qualmos are either wooden mannequins or masked clowns capering like highland monkeys. Would it surprise you to know that my mother was a qualmo? My father, a noble of the Clan Szim, took her to bed while campaigning in the lower isthmus. He took many captives for sacrifice to the Gods that season but my mother was too beautiful to be torn in pieces as food for their gustatory delight. She was to be, instead, the delight of a living star, a Nobleman of Szim. Seven years later, the qualmos rebelled again and he was there once more, taking me in with eyes like those of a breeder measuring a prime slinker at auction. His only daughter by the Nobless Iss died from a fever. He took me home with him to a manse of mottled stone and a different life as a daughter of a noble of Petzu Maal. My mother's tears fed the river and were dissipated into the southern sea.

I saw many things in the great stone city: pyramids made of blocks splashed red with the blood of captives, exotic spices for sale in

the leaf-roofed marketplace, jealousy and hatred disguised by soft words. Gifts of slaves
and blue-dyed cotton cloth when merchants
and nobles courted their peers for gain. I saw
great slinker lizards with venomous bile froth-
ing from their mouths, the smaller, evil cousins
of the great monsters which roamed the deep
bush. I watched ugly snarling slinkers, cages rattling about their dagger-toothed heads.
They were ridden by skull-helmed sons of
nobles clearing the streets of hungry, rioting
qualmos. I watched again with my father from
glazed tile balconies, eating honey-covered
meat as the mud-footed qualmos died, limbs
swollen twice their normal size from uncaged
slinker bites, their faces wretched masks of
hate and pain.

At twelve, I watched the spider assassins of
Kultzana kill my father with poison darts in
Great Willow square. The qualmos ran away.
His personal jaguar guards fought until the
end, surrounding him while he died an agonizing death by poison. Cracked, uneven flagstones ran with blood in a pattern that sug-
gested the characters I had learned from the
household priest. I painted a block-cloth of
those same characters along with a poem de-
scribing the incident and was celebrated for a
time by the city's literati.

At fourteen I secretly joined the cult of
Kultzana, the spider goddess. I learned the
art of subtle poison and my stepmother fell
ill from an indeterminable disease. She died
shortly thereafter. I inherited half of her prop-

erty, but my step-mother's relatives blackened my name. I was left with only the vetch I inhabit now.

I pray to the Great Mother Spider who sits at the heart of creation to help me to rise again, for the City is as cruel and as sure as She, and I was not made for a qualmo's life. I cast my web from Thee, O Mother! The degradation of my body and the proffering of my soul is a sacrifice for Thee!

Have I gained my wish?

On the day the western barbarian walked into my vetch, returning my gaze, brooding eyes watching mine as he drank. His face was chiseled marble browned by the sun. The Noble Tsherl spoke of the epic Danarl and the Blood Frogs with his cronies but his eyes shifted towards me and the barbarian. The room clouded with smoke from bamboo pipes filled with kusk. The stars grew bold above, flashing blue and white through the large open ceiling over the pond, while musicians blew reeds and struck leather-skinned tubes.

The barbarian sat there, unfashionably garbed, red haired, drinking my t'chal, immobile as a tree trunk but seething like a stone kettle on the boil. I could have hurled myself against that rock over and over, become the rug beneath his feet, but he would have only lifted his hand forever to his face, draining a bowl of fiery distillation while his other hand grasped the handle of his green sword like a lover. Can one be jealous of a sword? The Green City is jealous of everything not her and how could I not be jealous as well?

I had his fortune read in entrails and feathers. A dozen sorcerers took my jade tiles to send the spell of love-slavement but the enchantment shattered upon his damnable mystic sword. Finally, I bedded him. I dared not try the arts of seduction I had been given by the cult for he was too wild, too foreign. I used the older, truer arts of the woman. And it worked. In the movement of his limbs his great heart joined to mine in a way that of the Noble Tsherl could not. This barbarian, Faroj, opened to me. I saw his passion. He was one of those who thought birth nothing unless it allowed for a conquering spirit. He was one of those who sought glory for its own sake, power as a birthright granted by nature. I had been a conquest before. My pride was undamaged. We made love under the sweating stones of my bathhouse, in my cotton bed, on the blocks of my kitchen after I had driven the servants away. I gave everything to gain all but reserved one space, a space large enough for a spider only, in a corner of my throbbing heart.
He would not conquer that.

Eventually, I brought them together, the hot western barbarian from Kechna the Burning Waste, and the cold aristocrat of Petzu Maal, the Green City. Each had been content to ignore the other. Why did I do it? Perhaps to watch the steam and destruction that comes when lava pours from the mountain into the chill of a river? I cannot say, but I suspect the Great Goddess was working within me. My belly was a storm of excitement. I wanted Faroj but I would take either survivor.

Neither wasted their words.

"You have taken my seat, barbarian," said the Noble Tsherl.

"It is now my seat," said the barbarian.

"I am of the House of—"

"And I am of Kechna, a waste rider."

His manner was of a nobleman addressing a slinker groom.

A soft, heavy rain began to fall, and the stones outside the pavilion chattered death in droplets of pure water. Frogs croaked in time to our breathing.

"Then let us bring this poor tavern chair, stained with drink and the dirt of qualmos to a place where we can test our skill. The Lady of Lilypad Pleasure House will be glad to provide the grounds. Ta Bilin?"

My face was crimson. Tsherl was no barbarian and could see that I had woven this web. He might never forgive me. Tsherl accorded me the title of a noble lady. "Ta" was further reference to my current lack of high status and his cool anger.

"Of course, Noble Tsherl."

Faroj merely grunted assent and finished another bowl of fire.

The meeting was set for nine days later.

I trembled as I gave orders to ready the sacred enclosure. I then prayed to the gods that one would survive. Petzu Maal spent two days drinking the tale with their morning choklat, two days wagering on a winner, two days recounting the death tally of the great Tsherl of House Szim, two days weaving wild tales of the barbarian prowess of Faroj of the Burning Waste. On the day of the duel, all Petzu Maal chittered with expectation like a thicket of crickets. But not all in the Green City of Petzu Maal would be allowed to witness such a duel. Only nobles and guests of the participants, along with selected priests who would conduct the sacred rites, would be allowed into the sacred enclosure of Lilypad Pleasure House. Those few and the assassins of Kultzana who stood behind small openings in the walls of my Sacred enclosure, blow tubes loaded with death.

"What are our plans, O Great Mother?"

"The Goddess will decide at the moment, daughter."

"Who is to die?"

"The Goddess will decide. We await the outcome of the contest."

"What am I to do?"

"The will of the Goddess, of course."

The day of the duel dawned in humid heat. I walked into Lilypond Vetch and looked over the arrangements for the duel.

The priests of A'a and Xitil Xavo Kan were just finished rattling their gourds and clacking their thundersticks on the flagstones. There would be no slinker blood, nor the blood of pig or captive qualmo, spilled today. Today the blood of men would greet the nostrils of the gods, for all duels in Petzu Maal were to the death.

The Lord Tsherl of Clan Szim, named Wall of Petzu by the Holy Emperor, arrived. His jaguar guard whipped base qualmos from his path with leather thongs strung with onyx arrowheads. He wore the finest cotton robes, stained with bloody patterns of past duels and stitched with maidenhair depicting deeds of the Szim Clan. Tsherl refused my offer of berry juice and cake and stood talking quietly with his guards, holding his shield, stingray spine, and axe, cradling his weapons to his lean body like lovers.

Faroj entered the sacred enclosure, shaggy and muscular, breathing as he breathed, living as he lived. His eyes bore into mine and I shuddered. Whose will was this encounter, mine or his? A two-day growth of beard stubbled his cut jaw. What was I to him? A dark-haired beauty with golden eyes. Yes, I knew my own beauty, but before him I felt like an animal. I glanced at Tsherl again. To Tsherl I was a cool piece of stone, carven for his pleasure, held in permanence for his use. To him my beauty would never fade. But to Faroj, what was I?

The poison darts behind the grotto wall were ready. I had one last hope, one last demonstration of faith.

Were they for me?

"A'a shall judge!" Tsherl called out without looking at Faroj. He was ready to begin. The priests shuffled aside and their chanting died out of respect for the noble.

Faroj pulled his tunic of tanned slinker over his head, ruffling his red hair and revealing a chest blessed by A'a. A few of Faroj's desert comrades ringed him stoically, but inwardly seething with the same fire as their leader, barely holding it in check.

The stones of the rock garden sweated moisture around us.

A desert barbarian handed a length of slinker leather to Faroj and from it the wastelander slicked the deadly green two-handed weapon. Would it not shatter on Tsherl's glorious form? Green rock, green death, a city buried in moss. I prayed to the Great Goddess for guidance. I shivered in the heat of the steaming pond.

A'a rose a bit higher and a citrine light filtered slowly through the treetops changing the scene to an unreal tableau, like the death murals at Yellow Sanguinary, the secret cult grotto deep in the jungle.

Tsherl leaped from the flagstones to the sand. Faroj stepped down, holding the Ghost Sword. He held it like a plow, low. His leather-shod feet shuffled through the sand, toes gripping the earth.

Their fight began.

Later, they said that Mount Xaxos spouted plumes of molten black glass and red smoke at the time of the duel. They said the Gh'alos river became a road for giant turtles with screaming ghosts riding their backs. They said that storms formed above the enclosure and that A'a hid his face so long as sparks flew from the clash of weapons. These are all lies.

What happened was this: Tsherl, one of the greatest duelists of the Green City, leaped forward with blinding speed, guarding with his shield while thrusting with the deadly spine. Faroj turned his sword over, shielding his head and sliding to the right, just a foot. Tsherl brought his axe over his head and copper flashed one pure ray of sun, then descended.

But Faroj was not there.

Without flash or flourish the Ghost Sword was now buried in Lord Tsherl's head. I dropped the cup of t'chal Squash had given me to calm my nerves. The noble collapsed like a punctured bladder, spurting blood over the feet of the western barbarian where he stood breathing harsh breaths. Faroj's eyes returned to normal focus. The small openings in the grotto wall were silent. No darts sprang forth bringing anguished death. Squash and Vineblossom helped me to a private room and I became violently sick. Cheers erupted from the spectators behind me, even from some of Tsherl's friends, who applauded Faroj's skill.

I wept but did not know why.

And that is all that happened.

Faroj's fame grew. More of his kind followed from the west. He was appointed captain of the Emperor's Teeth, the city guards, and given charge of the security of the Green City. This was as high a title as anyone not from Petzu Maal could attain. Faroj filled the Emperor's Teeth with his cousins from the west and crushed insurrections in the surrounding countryside. He foiled more than one attempt upon the nobles and stopped three attempts upon his own life, each by the Szim clan. Faroj went unbothered by the priests of Xitol Xavo Kan. He was now held in high esteem by the qualmos who had mocked him. Even the middle castes and merchants sang his praises.

"Change is in the air. The Mimosa Throne is restless."

"How, Great Mother? Why?"

"Stay close to him, daughter of the spider. Be one with him."

It was during the next rainy season when things changed, when the air turned blue with water and the ground was a river of black mud, when the moss that gave the Green City its name flourished. Spring Sickness laid many in the city low, sweating with fever in their soaked cotton cots. Monster gronts as tall as temples came close to Petzu Maal and other towns and were only driven off with fire at the cost of many men. In the south the qualmos of the isthmus rose against their lords, pulling them from their beds in the night, killing them and devouring their stores like ravening slinkers. An army was sent south to quell the rebels. Faroj was given greater authority over the city in the absence of so many lords. Then came rumors of yet another army, half rebel, half wastelanders forming outside the borders of the Mimosa Empire. Qualmos in the city and surrounding area were stripped of their duties and sent to fight along with others from tributary cities. By then the forces guarding the Green City were mostly outlander mercenaries.

"They desecrate the temples, the holy squares, the streets themselves," the priests complained. "You strip our holy guards from us to fill their ranks. The temples have no protection."

"The Emperor needs every warrior upon the walls. They will serve Xitil Xavo Kan and Jhudru-ka there as well." Faroj spoke with the authority of one dressed in rich blue cotton, as the Emperor's Tooth. He unfolded the royal fan to signal the end of the audience. The priests walked away murmuring among themselves.

When summer came and the flies were dancing over what was left of our food, there was news from the west. The great army of outlanders and rebels had triumphed over Mimosa. They were marching toward Petzu Maal with all speed.

The Emperor came to Faroj and his brawny confidants. Summer sweat poured from his holy brow as he asked Faroj to lead the armies of the Mimosa Empire in a war to meet the western rebels and crush them. Faroj accepted with the condition that the powerful house of

Szim be exiled to their northern holdings. The Emperor made Faroj Axe of the West.

Within weeks the barbarians were at our gates and we were down to eating very little. Privation had no effect upon Faroj and his companions, who only grew stronger in forced asceticism. He had been distant from me as the crisis developed but now he came to me again, full of joy, like a youth. We twined together while the city starved. We drank t'chal while the qualmos drank mudwater. I shivered in his grasp. Sometimes I hated him. Sometimes I would have died for him.

I prepared a poison without telling the cult.

Change was coming. The city hummed with it. It had happened before. Everything would change except Petzu Maal. The Green City changed everything always to herself, for herself.

On the last day of summer, after the heat put frogs to sleep and sweated the stones dry, when tears dried on cheeks, the cult came, my own cult, assassinating several nobles and the high priests of three temples. I'm convinced that Faroj had no idea this would happen. They never informed me of their plans and disappeared as soon as the deeds were done. But there was no retribution, for Faroj was busy sending men to hold the gates open for his western brothers. These barbarians rode into town on unmuzzled slinkers, wreaking havoc with long blades and stone axes. Thick-legged qualmo women were raped before their dying mates. Those merchants who could pay for safety did not suffer. Nobles who acquiesced to the new reign were allowed to walk free, heads bowed in shame. Others were slaughtered. Faroj stood at the gate and greeted his wasteland brothers with open arms. They roared with joy at their conquest. Who had played with whom as a jaguar plays with a hare? Now, I knew. Now, we all knew.

None of my things or properties were touched. My jewels, sacred screens, and choklat fields were sacrosanct by his order. Faroj found me necessary.

One day Faroj had the Emperor and his family killed. Their hides flapped in the breeze showering the awed crowd with drops of formerly sacred blood. Priests of A'a, acknowledging the will of the gods, consecrated Faroj Emperor of the Coral Sun, seating him on the Mimosa Throne in barbarian splendor.

"The qualmos wished it so. You think they loved their Emperor but they did not." Faroj observed me with cool green eyes.

I did not think they loved him, but I replied, "The qualmos wish for roast mammoth meat too. Will you provide that? What if they cheered your death and the death of every emperor?"

The Kechna, now Emperor of the Mimosa Empire, wrapped his heavy hands around my limbs, pulling me into my candlelit inner chamber. Roaring with laughter he shouted to the gods. "Let them eat beans and corn. Meat is for us, not them!"

Then, as so often before, our bodies were one. Outside, Petzu Maal burned with the fever of dynastic change.

I filled his bedchamber with my body while my mind quailed.

Now, every night I prepare a poison for his cup and every night I pour it out. Sometimes I love him, sometimes I would slit his throat in slumber. Sometimes I would poison him, sometimes I would drink the poison myself.

I am with child now. I, daughter of a nobleman and a qualmo woman, the owner of a pleasure house, the consort of an emperor, am to be a mother. Every evening he tells me stories of his youth. I stare at the ceiling of our bedchamber whereon a jaguar eating a maiden has been painted. He sings drunken songs of the Burning Waste and tells me his stories every night.

II.

A dozen sweating qualmos were taking their noonday cornmash and beer under the merciless sun of Trejtal at the edge of the Burning Waste. They sat on rude benches spooning mashed corn and karo into their mouths under a cotton awning which stretched between the mudbrick columns of a vetch called the Crimson Slinker. The Crimson Slinker was decorated with a depiction of that lizardlike beast painted crudely on the flaking mud of the tavern in the color of old blood. Scratching out a living in the scorched hell that A'a had created at the western edge of the Empire was difficult for the thick qualmo. His noon meal and a cup or two of sour beer helped him complete that work. The qualmo preferred the cooler hours of late afternoon when the god grew sleepy. After A'a dipped into the somnambulant western horizon, slinker hunting, gathering of tubers and corn, and wrangling vicious beasts of the desert grew easier.

As they ate, sweat dripped from mud colored faces into bowls and cups, pooling in the corners of baked tile plates. Hats made from elsh fronds, strong as cotton, hung low over their brows while muscular jaws masticated. Lean limbs covered in dried mud prevented sunburn but the cracked skin was already black. The qualmos stank of sweat and dust.

A green arjoz bird flopped noisily to the top of a crumbling column nearby, eyeing the meager leavings on a clay plate. Elbows moved in time with the clacking of wooden spoons. A doorway cut crookedly in the cracked wall of the vetch was a gaping wound bandaged by two hanging sheets of dirty leather.

Now, the qualmos squinted over their bowls at a sudden smudge of reddish-brown on the horizon. The smudge resolved into dots and the dots into figures. The qualmos did not blink. Spoons moved from mouth to bowl again and again. Their eyes never quit the nearing figures.

Xatos squinted at the yellow powder spiraling into the sky behind stick figures bobbing on the horizon. Tall plumes of dust scattered and disappeared courtesy of the ever-present breeze blowing in hot from the waste. Ragged fronds at the edge of Xatos's hat nodded in time to a drumming of the sands which he felt deep in his breast. Xatos shoved the last spoonfuls of karo into his mouth, drained his wooden cup, belched, and rose slowly to his feet. A handful of riders appeared above the gully separating the Crimson Slinker from the waste proper. The figures appeared piecemeal, head, bodies, then serpentine lizards, recklessly driving on toward the vetch where the qualmos sat eating and drinking. Xatos could see them better now: pointed boots flapping, fired glass armor glinting in the setting sun, each bobbing to his own rythym.

Four riders came. They stopped inside the gate of the tavern raising a wave of dust. They tied their squabbling mounts to the post and stalked into the courtyard, kicking the occupants of the best table to the ground.

Xatos looked at his neighbor nearby. Kechna, mouthed the man. Barbarian ghosts. The riders sat and loudly ordered beer and food. They were clearly used to the weight and heat of their fired ceramic armor. Those qualmos who had been kicked to the ground crawled away. Xatos moved his bench back, expecting he would have to run. The nervous tavern slave poured again when Xatos held out his cup.

Xatos watched the four who had fallen to arguing. One slapped a bag on the table.

"Lord Andoh will be satisfied," he said.

"The Lord wanted his head," coughed another, a bushy-headed bravo with red hair hanging halfway down his back. He quenched his dusty throat, drinking the dregs left by the expelled qualmos.

The leader, a man with a red quill projecting from his leather cap, pointed a calloused, sunburned finger at the speaker. "The Great Shade of the Burning Waste will be happy to receive the Holy Visage. The head can wait. We need more men. Fetch Kar, Tun-dal, Llemk—"

"That wild ghost is a desert demon," the third put in, looking over his shoulder. "I saw him leap behind the rocks after we grabbed the old man and—"

"It's hot," said the fourth. He dropped his flint axe head down on the dirt with a thump and turned his pilfered cup upward, thick moustache jutting to either side. Liquid poured around his lips and down his brown-blue fired armor. Wiping his mouth and forehead on a yellowed buff cotton sleeve he blurted out, "Forget the wild man, let us take the mask to the temple and shed these protections!"

Xatos chewed a last bit of mashed corn and looked to the slinkers tied to the gate. They were squabbling with each other, snapping as much as their gabbles allowed, red stripes flashing over slick green skin, long lizard necks swaying from side to side. These were fast mounts of the waste, thought Xatos, bred by the barbarian ghosts for speed, durability, and toughness. They were treacherous, difficult for qualmos to handle. Xatos had ridden a ghost slinker when he worked a herd of the quarrelsome beasts in his youth. These were quality mounts.

Pale dust trailed just below the horizon. Soon he was able to make out a fifth rider against the washed-out distance. Xatos watched him ride up to the rail without hurry. He tied off his mount and ambled into the baking courtyard. A long spear projected from the saddle of his restless slinker. But he left that obsidian tipped death to rest in its sheath, carrying instead a two-handed sword made of a single length of sinuous green stone, an edged serpent slung over his back. Another Kechna, with a tangle of red hair blown by the wind. He wore no hat. His hawk's nose and chiseled cheeks bore the marks of the sun god's anger. A red beard hung a hand's length below his chin. He wore a brown tunic of woven elshfrond and boots of grontskin. His green eyes were a hardness fixed on a horizon beyond the vision of others.

The bravos slid from their benches as the stranger approached, hands falling near to axe, flint dagger, obsidian short double spears, battle-sword, and mountainwood buckler.

"What do you want Krokoa?" said the leader. "You walk as a ghost among ghosts. No man of your people remains to help you."

"And we have given your women to those who tend our slinkers," said the fifth rider.

"Where are your men, dogs of Andoh? They don't appear on the horizon behind me," said the red-haired stranger.

Xtolt, leader of the bravos and commander of Lord Andoh's temple guard, slapped his chest, causing the fire-hardened armor to tinkle. "They are dealing with a rabble who challenged Lord Andoh's right to a temple treasure."

Xtolt clenched his fist in the air. The other three came forward and adopted a semi-circle around the tall stranger. The remaining qualmos abandoned their seats with incontinent speed to hide in the shadows of the vetch. They still chewed their food, slowly, with wide eyes. Life may be wasted but food could not be so wasted.

The stranger cast hooded eyes upon the cotton bag on the table. Xtolt placed his buckler hand on the bag and the other on the wooden hilt of his sword. "That rogue shaman no longer needs this. His head will sit a pole in the temple garden."

Eyes of green jasper followed Xtolt's hand. The stranger smiled. "You do not have the head of the blessed shaman Elyos, though he is dead. The thirsty sands of the Burning Waste drank the blood of the men you left to take it."

"That demon. I saw him. He's the one that leapt—"

The fourth bravo never finished his revelation. In the space of half a breath the red-haired stranger with tribal markings belonging to an extinct people stepped forward and drew the sword hanging in a grontskin sheath down his back. It slid through leather straps and moved, a green arc of extermination, through the arm of the fourth bravo before the stone axe could begin to be lifted. The arm dropped to the ground, fingers still writhing around the haft. A thin whistling scream sounded from the fourth bravo's lips.

The qualmos held their breath. Food dropped from their open mouths as the other two members of Lord Andoh's temple guard were moved to action. Two obsidian spear tips sprang out to strike as the stranger leaped over the agonized figure of the maimed and dying bravo. The first was thrust aside by the serpentine blade of stone, but the second pierced the stranger's side and was pulled out in a gout of blood. The clawed hand of the stranger grabbed the haft of the spear as it was pulled from his side and green death circled to cut halfway through the pulsing neck. A cactus-haired jaw pointed at the sky while a lifeless sack collapsed under it.

Qualmos broke for openings in the vetch walls. The weapon thrust once, twice, thrice, and the stranger danced a staccato tarantella of avoidance. Then the sword sang once again through the dry air of the cursed waste. The third bravo watched his nose fly away to land in the yellow sand, a treat for lizards and flies. Clacking thrusts and retreats followed in the course of a few bubbling breaths and the third bravo was down, red holes making a bullfrog's throat of his face.

"Kill me," he said from his place in the sand.

"A'a burn your body to ash, brave warrior, and your soul reborn." The green sword passed through the man again. His stomach was now a punctured waterskin.

Xatos's youth had been spent in the waste, raiding and stealing slinkers, fornicating, drinking fermented drinks. Now he was past his prime but something in his inner being called upon him to act. His grandmother had been of the Screaming Tree before they were destroyed. Xatos watched the tall redheaded stranger with a beard slaughter the temple bravos of Lord Andoh.

Xtolt watched as, in the space of a few breaths, Alt, Gurh, and Tin Pwul the Axe, were cut down by the tall stranger with the green blade. He was not afraid. He had taken the temple torc of Lord Andoh, Wall of the West, servant of the Mimosa Throne. His duty was to deliver the holy Mask of A'a to that Lord or suffer a loss of soul. He would miss the jokes and drinking skills of his personal bodyguard but they were caterpillars eaten by the birds of fate. He, Xtolt, would deliver the Mask and then disembowel this last member of the heretical Screaming Tree Clan. His blade, Black Wand, shards of razor onyx set in the hardest ironwood, would sing. It had taken dozens of warriors and hundreds of shrieking qualmos. Now, the stranger would sleep in the House of Denuu forever, ashamed to be reborn. If the Wand needed aid then the flies of destruction would be there. They never missed. Xtolt was sure of his own skill.

He took up the cotton bag containing the Mask of A'a. He ran into the vetch. Shadows scattered as the qualmos scurried from their hiding places. Xtolt kicked open a reed door and exited the drunken-walled tavern in the rear. Instead of running into the sparsely weeded ground away from the waste, he climbed a wall quickly and jumped onto the low roof, careful not to dislodge the broken terra cotta littering the surface. Xtolt lay still.

A lone, grizzle-bearded qualmo approached the barbarian, pointing to his side where a wide rivulet of blood ran its course down his pelvis and leg. The other qualmos had fled but this one walked slowly towards the stranger with the green blade. The blunt-faced peasant, a decade past his prime, pointed at the wound in the stranger's side. He offered a cotton rag. Faroj allowed him to stuff the cloth into the wound. He looked to the qualmo who pointed silently to the darkened door of the vetch and then to the slanted roof above. The stranger motioned towards the door and went to stand in the shaded section of the vetch where the awning hung over the porch. He melted into the wall and stood silent. The qualmo disappeared through the doorway.

A few breaths later, there was a rattle from the rear of the vetch. Xtolt leaped from a high gable to the front of the vetch, tucking into a roll, then regaining his feet. He kept his shield but his quilled cap flew from his head to settle over the still face of bravo number three. The captain did not wait but felt for the jade mask still safely bagged and tucked into his belt. He ran for his slinker, thinking that the red-haired man had climbed the roof behind him.

Xtolt heard a cry and turned to find his foe only a dozen feet to his rear. In a moment he altered course, rolling to the side over his shield, drawing Black Wand as he rose. The barbarian drove past him and turned, cutting off any access to the slinker tied to the heavy post below.

Who was behind the vetch, thought Xtolt? A stupid qualmo from inside, trying to escape. He had heard the noise and acted too soon. The leader of Lord Andoh's temple guards stood erect. Time to kill this ghost man of a ghost tribe. No matter that they were both Kechna, this was the way of honor. Lord Andoh would have to wait upon his prize.

A'a hung high in the sky casting his withering breath upon the land while time stood still for a moment. Then the clacking of blade against blade was as that of the irontree in the desert storm. Gasp against gasp, shuffling sand as feet moved in the deadly stillness of the world.

"Who are you?" heaved Xtolt. A shard of Black Wand fell away. The captain retreated. I cannot defeat him, thought Xtolt. Who trained him? As the thought subsided, Xtolt released the outer strap of his shield, leaving his forearm tight in the central leather band. With two fingers he nimbly pulled a pair of sharp flies from the inside edge of the shield where they were gummed securely by a poisonous paste. Moving through a series of disconcerting moves he released the flies of destruction, flinging them at the unarmored chest before him.

For half a second there was the sun and the whistle of the flies as they left his hand. Then a shadow appeared under Xtolt's extended shield and the head and feet of a qualmo were visible holding an obsidian knife in one hand and a wooden plate scavenged from the abandoned tables in the other. The flies embedded themselves in the plate and stood quivering, thwarted from delivery of their virulent message.

Xatos lunged forth with his knife severing the ends of the two fingers which sent the darts. Xtolt, ignoring the pain, lashed out with Black Wand, knocking the wooden plate from the qualmo's hand. The barbarian did not wait for Xtolt to cut down Xatos but stepped forward to plunge the glinting green blade into the captain's exposed breast, cracking fired armor. Xtolt's spine arched as the green blade passed through his back.

"Who are you?" said the captain.

Eyes as green as the blade that killed him peered down. The barbarian pulled the cotton sack free of the fine bead belt as Xtolt's nerveless fingers lost their grip upon Black Wand. "My name is Faroj of the Screaming Tree," rasped the barbarian. "And this is the Ghost Sword."

Xatos watched Faroj pull the Ghost Sword from the dead captain's breast. Rivulets of blood ran its length and the blade stood winking in the light of A'a, red and green. Watching Faroj for any objection, Xatos gingerly reached down to take Xtolt's fine bead belt and the smaller pouch that depended from it. Within were copper tiles and round ivory brain pearls of the rare Yg. "Why should it go to waste?" said Xatos. "We can dine on this and sleep on feathers for a month."

"Dine?" Faroj asked.

"Always consider the future. My grandmother dreamed about you. She was of the Screaming Tree." Xatos pointed at the tribal markings adorning the barbarian's chest and upper arms: a great tree of the waste, pierced by mouths in many places.

"Where is she now?"

"She died at the time of the Wandering Star."

"That is when I was born," said Faroj. He made to walk away, but stopped. "You may have saved my life. Ask what you will."

Xatos grinned and held up the belt and pouch. "But I will follow you," he said. "You should seek a healer."

"Afterward." Faroj turned and walked toward the line of slinkers. "Come, then."

Xatos followed. "But I have no slinker to ride behind you."

"No." Faroj pointed to the tethered beasts. "You have four."

Forty miles into the Burning Waste, in a place cursed by A'a, a place made into a clay oven for men, Faroj knelt before a low cairn while Xatos watched from a near sandy ridge.

Beside the tall qualmo a staked line of five slinkers grazed moodily upon sparse clumps of green stems. The animals desired flesh. The qualmo watched the hazy horizon for massive gronks covered with yellow dust, for stealthy groats, for hell-scorpions and sand shamblers, for the dust of deadly tribesmen of the waste. But mostly he watched Faroj present the Mask of A'a to the dead shaman Elyos, laying it gently upon the mass of crumbled stone with which he had covered the lifeless body.

Faroj's sculpted form moved in odd, contrite ways. Xatos felt the barbarian was talking to the shaman but his simple mind could not imagine the context of such projected emotion.

Below on the rock-strewn plain Faroj knelt and spoke. "Elyos, I have avenged you and recovered the sacred mask. I would hang it once again in the hidden temple but you are not there. The last of our people are slain."

Faroj placed the carven jade visage on the rough mound he had gathered. Overcome by fatigue, he slept next to the cairn. Xatos waited patiently above. The grizzled qualmo thought he could make out a figure next to Faroj at dusk, but it could have been a trick of the desert light. He, too, slept.

The next morning, Xatos awakened stiff and shivering in the wasteland dawn where the bullying twins, cold and heat, alternated night and day. The slinkers were snapping in their gabble-cages, setting a mood for the morning. Faroj appeared over the top of the ridge as

Xatos was beating the slinkers into order. He fed them gobbets of dried meat.

Faroj stared into a distant horizon as he described his evening in a husky voice. "Elyos came to me in a dream and presented the Mask of A'a. 'There is no longer a tribe for the mask to guard,' he said. 'All of the Screaming Tree walk the path with me in the Darklands. Now, the mask will guard you, Faroj. You carry the destiny of the people.'"

The qualmo's brows rose quizzically as he shared his own meager breakfast.

"What did he mean?" asked Xatos.

"That is for another time."

Xatos thought that maybe the brawny warrior might not know the meaning himself. He changed the subject. "Faroj, where did you get the Ghost Sword?"

"Another time, Xatos. Now, we will make plans to kill Lord Andoh."

Xatos did not allow his brows to rise. Instead, pointing to Faroj's bleeding side, he said, "Your wound is open again."

Faroj made a face of irritation and chewed his meat slowly. "We will find a healer. Then we will make plans to kill Lord Andoh. We will need help."

Xatos snorted. "Do you think so?"

III.

This story he told me. This and many others.

Sometimes when the wet closeness of Petzu Maal and its priests, thieves, scheming nobles, mudfaced qualmos, and savage barbarians clothe me in layers of despair, I walk the three hundred steps to the top of the temple of Xitil Xavo Kan, above the fog. There I watch the countless cookfires of the Green City. The smoke rises above stone and umber clay tiles, crooked arthritic fingers in the sky. To the north I see the humped and ragged shapes of the Skull Mountains, to the south the Sobbing Mire stretches endlessly to the Great Sea. Even now I think I hear the wailing cry of a rogue gront as he stalks through the muddy fens seeking a meal. But it is my imagination only, for they are beyond earshot. Still, I watch the haze above the mire and wonder. And dream.

What do I do above the steaming city? Do you think I look down on them all because I am now the mistress of Petzu Maal? Me, the one they call the Whore Queen, consort of a barbarian Emperor.

The wasteland savage and his whore.

I do not come to gloat. I come to breathe fresher air. Sometimes I come to cast the bones and hope for a different future. My maiden escort and bodyguards shuffle carefully behind me as I climb the stone steps. They know better than to speak when I am in this mood. But now they stand aside and I hear boots of grontskin coming up stone steps. His is a heavy tread. My rough lover appears and orders a chair brought beside my own. As he turns his broad back I see, again, the green mask woven into the braids of his red hair. A'a accuses me from the spine of my lover and Emperor and I turn my head away.

Faroj sits a while in silence. My fingers travel over his many scars. He is pensive, distant, rarely ever near. He casts his mind back to the past, drawing me with him as he begins to speak. Having conquered the greatest empire in the world, what is he to do next? What is the meaning of it all? He wants our child, still in the womb, to hear. Does he fear he will not be here to tell the story himself? Hate and love, the two sides of Mount Makos. The gods care not for our wants. They feed like leather-winged raptors on our passions.

Faroj begins to tell me of his past and now I must listen once again.

RETVRN

SCHUYLER HERNSTROM
thune's vision
This book was my only company in a lonely time. Simply xcellent!
Lone Wolf
A classic collection.
Three new fictions.
Monkeyshines.

Pilum Press Trade Edition
Available wherever fine books
are sold and from
www.pilumpress.com